MCP

03052877

LT
Gill   Gill, Judy

A harvest of jewels

MAY 2 7 2003

FEB 1 9 2004	DATE DUE		
MAY 6 2004			

A Harvest of Jewels

A HARVEST
OF
JEWELS

Judy Gill

Thorndike Press • Chivers Press
Waterville, Maine USA   Bath, England

This Large Print edition is published by Thorndike Press®, USA and by Chivers Press, England.

Published in 2003 in the U.S. by arrangement with Judy Gill.

Published in 2003 in the U.K. by arrangement with the author.

U.S. Hardcover   0-7862-5081-X   (Candlelight Series)
U.K. Hardcover   0-7540-7201-0   (Chivers Large Print)

The text of this Large Print edition is unabridged.

Other aspects of the book may vary from the original edition.

Set in 16 pt. Plantin by Liana M. Walker.

Printed in the United States on permanent paper.

British Library Cataloguing-in-Publication Data available

Library of Congress Cataloging-in-Publication Data

Gill, Judy (Judy Griffith)
    A harvest of jewels / by Judy Gill.
        p.   cm.
    ISBN 0-7862-5081-X (lg. print : hc : alk. paper)
    1. Children — Institutional care — Fiction. 2. Children
with disabilities — Fiction. 3. British Columbia — Fiction.
4. Indian children — Fiction. I. Title.
PR9199.3.G5298 H37 2003
    813'.54—dc21   2002043062

In Memory of my father,
ROBERT LYON GRIFFITH
Who also saw jewel trees.

ONE

'Karen, it's no good! You can't go on like this. You needed a break even before you came here and for the past six months I've watched you going further and further downhill and deeper into a depression that could only culminate in a breakdown like this. Most of it's my fault; I thought I could catch it before something like this happened, but I got too busy and this is the result. You're worn out, physically, mentally and emotionally. I'm ordering you to take at least a month's vacation, and I'd like to see you not work for a year.'

Karen Jamison's voice, hoarse from the harsh use it had just been given, shook when she replied to Dr Porter. 'I can't! Even if I could afford to take a month off, I couldn't afford to go away and I'd go crazy staying in the house. It's all I can do to go home when I'm off duty. I have no savings left and I have to eat!'

'Go home to your parents, Karen,' came the gentle suggestion. 'You know they want you to.'

'Oh, Doctor,' the girl moaned, rocking her pale head back and forth against the chair in her agitation, 'it's impossible . . . impossible!' Her voice rose again toward hysteria and the doctor placed a quieting hand on the too-thin shoulder.

'All right, Karen, easy now. Let the shot I gave you take over. I'm going to drive you home now and put you to bed for twenty-four hours. Would you like me to ask one of your neighbours to stay with you, or to check in now and then?'

'No . . .' Karen allowed herself to be pulled from the chair. Her muscles were limp and heavy. She felt sick. 'I don't know any of the neighbours.'

Driving into the yard of the small bungalow with the cherry tree in the back, Carol Porter said, 'You've lived here for three and a half years, Karen. Why don't you know any of the neighbours?'

'I . . . haven't had time to make friends. Besides, they're all elderly. That's why I stayed after . . . that's why I haven't moved.'

'Foolish, Karen, foolish.'

'But necessary,' came the weary reply.

'We'll talk more about that later.' Dr Porter put on the parking brake and unclipped her seat belt. 'I'll stay with you tonight, and no arguments.'

Over Karen's weak protests, she took the girl inside, undressed her and put her to bed in her darkened room where she lay with weak tears running down her face until at last she slipped into much needed sleep.

Dr Porter wandered through the little house for some moments, picking up photos, putting them down, shaking her head and at last roamed out into the shady yard. A short, stout figure in an overly-bright print dress, she looked more like someone's grandmother, which indeed she also was, than the competent physician in charge of a geriatric hospital where she had so recently come across the tail end of the scene which had brought her here.

She was unsure just what had taken place before the raised voices, loud and stormy weeping and then the deep silence which followed the pistol-shot crack of a hand on a face had sent her next door to the office of the hospital matron.

'What's up?' she had asked, seeing the flushed face, the tight mouth of the prim Miss Carson, and the white, shaking nurse with a livid hand-print on her cheek, slumped weeping hopelessly in a chair.

'She insulted Miss Haskins' family terribly!' snapped the matron, 'and now she refuses to apologize. She screamed at me the way she had screamed at them and I slapped her! That girl will go, Doctor, or I will! We cannot have the staff insulting the patients' families!'

'Of course not,' agreed the doctor, trying to soothe the not unnaturally ruffled feelings of Miss Carson. 'I'll handle this. Karen, come with me.' She had taken the unresisting nurse into her own office, talked for a few minutes, administered the injection, and then listened while Karen tearfully tried to explain.

'You didn't see them, Doctor! She didn't see them! They were horrible! The whole time I've been here I've had to tell that poor little woman that there were no visitors for her . . . again . . . Everyday! She never complained, just smiled and sat there, blind, unable to move without help and when I'd peep in later, she'd be crying soundlessly and I thought my heart would break! And the day after she dies, here they are, digging through her things, demanding what little jewelery she had in the safe, counting the stones, wrangling over who gets what and when two of them broke a necklace, one she had liked better than any, I started to tell them off!'

'And you just couldn't quit?' Dr Porter was right. Karen had been unable to stop. She had just raged on and on and on and when she was removed, taken to the matron's office, she found she still couldn't quit. Not until the crack of Miss Carson's hand on her face had sent her reeling into the chair where Dr Porter had found her and, when she started weeping, she was unable to stop that.

The injection had helped there, recalled Carol Porter, 'Mother' to three young adults and 'Granny' to seven children. She sighed softly and lowered her tired body into a lawn chair. What could be done about that poor, broken child in there? It had been against her better judgement to let her work in the geriatric hospital and she now wished desperately that she had listened to that judgement instead of thinking she could keep a weather eye out for serious trouble and catch it before it erupted. She hoped that by talking to that sour matron she could salvage Karen Jamison's career, but as Miss Carson had said when Dr Porter took Karen on the staff, 'An unstable nurse has no place in this profession.'

Quite right, she reflected, pulling a stool

closer to rest her swollen feet, but Karen, whom she had known for many years, whom she had watched grow, whose joys and griefs she had shared, was not unstable; she was just at the end of her rope. It was no wonder, either!

When, six months ago, Karen had come back to nursing after nearly three years away, she had begged for a job where Dr Porter worked. Well, she had been given it, and had done it well, but today it had come to an end. Even if, for the sake of Karen's health, Carol hadn't made her leave, the matron would certainly not have her back!

It wasn't only today's scene that made the doctor sure of that, but the fact that Miss Carson had a down on any and all pretty girls, and one with pale, almost white hair — platinum, didn't they call it? — and pansy-brown eyes, a striking combination, especially with that unconscious air of tragedy about her, was simply too much for Miss Carson.

So what to do?

Dr Porter sat pondering for some time. She rose at length and went inside, a more purposeful swing to her step, checked her friend and patient then picked up the telephone. Shortly thereafter she was chatting

and laughing easily, then speaking seri-
ously, listening, and finally, still cradling
the telephone against her shoulder, pinned
by her chin, she depressed the button, and
dialled again, reading the number off the
card as she did so.

'Hello . . . Frank?' The voice at the other
end acknowledged that she was speaking to
him and she said, 'Carol Porter, here,
Frank.'

'Karen?' Karen's father was immediately
alert.

'She's all right. But she's had enough.
More than enough and I've told her she
has to take at least a month off and then
find a different job.' The doctor went on to
give an edited version of the day's events
and ended by asking, 'can you run to
paying half her hotel, meals and transportation costs?'

'Half of it? Good God, Carol! I'm paying
for all of it!'

'No, Frank. She needs her independence. When she wakes up, she's going to
be bitterly ashamed of falling apart the way
she did, and if we take all her self-respect,
her independence, at once, she may never
recover. She won't even know you're in on
it, paying half. I've already made the arrangements with Lois Granger who runs

13

Cassiare House. So it's all O.K. with you, then?'

'Of course, Carol . . . and thanks. Want to talk to Di? She's nearly breaking both our necks trying to hear.'

After a few moments of pleasant conversation, Diane Lytell said with a hint of a tremor in her voice, 'Thank you, Carol, for looking after our girl for us. I just wish she'd let . . . us . . .' her voice broke.

'Diane . . . Diane, it's not that she doesn't love you or need your support. She just has to do it all on her own. There's a streak of independence in most of us, and like any hurt animal, Karen needs to lick her wounds in private.'

'It . . . it's more than that, Carol . . .' There was a frown in Diane's voice. 'She's afraid . . . of something. I could see it those few minutes she was in the house at Christmas, and I've sensed it each time we were over to visit her.'

'It might be that she's afraid to let herself lean, for fear she'll fall into too many pieces to be put back together, or maybe she's afraid to feel love for fear it'll be snatched away, too. We can only wait, Di, and give her what support she'll accept. Good-bye for now, my dear. I'll be in touch. My love to the others . . .'

'Cassiare House?' Karen was sitting up in bed fingering a slice of toast from her tray. The doctor explained:

'It's a resort up the coast. There's golfing, tennis, swimming, boating, dancing, movies and nice, cool quiet walks through the forest. It'll do you good and is quite inexpensive. There's no room or maid service, no table service. All meals are served buffet style and the guests are responsible for keeping their own rooms done up.' She named the cost, which included transportation, and was gratified by the faint spark of interest shown in Karen's eyes.

'At that price I think I could manage a couple of weeks,' she said tentatively, still not convinced.

'You need a month! Your dad would help, Karen, if you asked . . . or even hinted . . .'

'No! I couldn't.' Karen swallowed rapidly, choked.

'Then three weeks, Karen? Surely three weeks wouldn't totally break the bank?'

'Well . . . not really . . . but . . .'

'But you don't have a job to come back to? Is that all it is?'

She nodded. 'I know I can't go back to geriatrics and I won't go into an active hospital! It may take a bit of time to find a private case, assuming, of course, that yesterday didn't foul things up completely!'

'You'll get an excellent reference from me, and from your training hospital and if you'll go for three weeks, I'll keep my eyes and ears open for some kind of a job for you.'

'All right, Dr Porter. And . . . how do I say thanks for all you've done for me?'

'You just enjoy Cassiare House. That's all I want from you. It'll do you so much good,' the doctor reiterated. 'Filled with young people, activities, noise . . .' She smiled, thinking how hard it was to sound enthusiastic about a place she could only see herself in with a degree of horror.

'And . . . and . . .' Karen's face twisted. 'There are no . . . no . . .'

'None, Karen. None at all. But it's time you got over that, my dear. You can't spend the rest of your life like this!'

'I have to! I have to!' Karen wailed. 'I can't bear it. I can't face them!'

'All right, Karen,' said Dr Porter evenly. 'No one's going to force you. You will when you feel you can, just as you'll be

16

able to go home again when you feel you can.'

'I went home at Christmas . . .' Karen shuddered. 'I won't go again, ever! You don't know, Doctor! You can't possibly know . . . I lasted exactly one hour and ten minutes and then I had to leave even knowing I was spoiling Christmas for them all by running away. I'd have spoiled it more by staying!'

'You didn't spoil it for them by running away. They all know how hard it must have been for you. Your family loves you, Karen.'

'Yes! Yes! But if they knew . . . they'd hate me! If Johnny knew . . . Oh, God! They'd all hate me!' Her face was contorted, her hands twisted into hard knots and her eyes squeezed tightly shut against some terrible scene visible only to herself.

'If Johnny knew what? What would make him hate you? Answer me, Karen! Tell me now! What?' This time, oh, please, this time let her get through to the girl, let her get into the mind and heart of Karen and help her! 'What have you done to make Johnny hate you?'

'No, no, no, I didn't do it! I won't do it! No, no, no, no, oh, leave me alone! Go away! I didn't! I didn't!'

17

Dr Porter quickly gave her patient another injection and waited until it took effect before going to the next house and speaking to the old couple who were only too happy to check in on 'that poor little Mrs Jamison . . .'

It was pouring rain, and had been since she left Vancouver, when Karen first sighted Cassiare House from the heaving deck of the charter boat which made the weekly run to the resort. The ship's whistle blared two short blasts and the bow nosed in toward a wharf slung by a slanted ramp to high mounds of craggy rock, brown and slick with shiny weeds while higher up grew dismal gray moss, superceded by scraggy little shrubs and creepers clinging to crannies. Above all that, in mind-boggling profusion, were trees and trees and trees as high as the eye could see until they were lost in the tattered grey clouds which hung grimly, drizzling their depressing moisture from the summit of the mountain to a sea pockmarked with rain.

Karen stood alone near the bow and pulled her scarf tighter around her hair, muttering to herself, 'Good for me? Like castor oil!' Behind her, the laughter of the crowd of young people, like her, in their twenties mostly, shattered into excited gabble as they crammed around the windows of the saloon to rub at the steam and peer upward, as she was, at the bulk of Cassiare House.

It was a wide low structure sitting snugly in a dip of land, the sides of which swooped up and back in broad swaths of dark grass, glistening now with rain, and merging eventually with the wall of the sodden forest. There was a large, glassed-in front porch with lights glowing around its outline, and from this, through double doors, appeared a figure carrying an umbrella and walking quickly toward the boat which was now docking.

Lois Granger soon mustered the guests and their luggage, ushering them up the slick path and into the warm, dry lounge where sat the departing guests and their baggage, ready to board the boat for their return trip.

In surprisingly short time this exchange of guests had been completed and Karen watched through dripping window panes the departure of her last means of escape from a vacation she was becoming increasingly sure she would end up regretting with all her heart. But, she consoled herself, there would be a boat out in one week, and if she really couldn't stand it, she would leave on that boat.

During that week, while she waited for the ship which would take her away from this place, she learned two facts. The first of these was that a resort which catered to young couples did not truly welcome a single woman, especially a widow. The men who were pleasant to her often earned the displeasure of their wives or girl friends who had, after all, come on vacation to enjoy the company of their mates . . . and a third wheel was not to be encouraged.

The second fact was that for the first time in over three years she cared, and wished desperately for someone . . . not just *the* one . . . but anyone who could make her feel less lonely.

It was easier to go for long, solitary walks through the cool forest trails that Dr Porter had mentioned than it was to sit back, alone, always alone, and watch happy couples playing tennis, cards, dancing, dining at intimate little tables or in large, laughing, *even-numbered* groups. Karen felt old, tired, and miserably, frighteningly lonely!

She took her meals with Lois Granger, that kind woman sensing somehow what

Karen was feeling, and trying to make up, even to the extent of inviting her to visit during the long, boring evenings which with Lois, became much less so. Karen was sitting at the little table she shared with Lois waiting for her hostess one evening almost a week after she had arrived, when she sensed someone was looking at her. She did not turn, sure that if she did, it would be Ralph Hodges, one of the married men who persistently paid her attention when his wife was out of sight. Lois arrived and they chatted through their meal, at the end of which time Karen retired to her room and a book, to free Lois to do something on her own for a change. That she was right in assuming Lois had things to do was obvious, for her hostess made no demur when Karen excused herself.

The following morning after breakfast Karen walked slowly to a headland where the fresh breeze took the warmth out of the sun which had shone, as Lois had promised, for most of the week Karen had been there.

The cliff-top was carpeted with thick, shaggy moss. Tall clumps of waving, coarse grass studded it here and there, and on the very brink, where Karen now headed to enjoy the scented breeze wafting in from the blue water below her, stood a gnarled arbutus tree, that coastal oddity which grows on wind-swept crags and sheds its paper-thin red bark in delicate piles under its twisted limbs.

The tide was running out as she arrived and sat on the moss to lean against the smooth trunk of the green-leafed arbutus. As the water poured out of the arm which led off the main inlet it was caught in the bottleneck of rock and island and whipped into rapids which boiled and frothed as the forces of nature drew out the waters of the inlet, sucking them through the gap in a roaring, rushing maelstrom of foam and spume and black walls of eddies spinning, tossing, writhing! As she got to her feet, releasing her hold on the tree, leaning, tipping, being drawn into the morass below her she was caught, held, pulled roughly back and roundly scolded.

'Little fool! That whole pad of moss could have let go at any minute, spilling you into the chuck! Haven't you got more sense than that? What's the matter with your head!' Strong hands shook her hard and as they did so, Karen's hair flew back from her face. The man gasped and let her go as if he had been burned.

Her enormous brown eyes were empty, devoid of life, of hope. Her face seemed slack and without personality behind it. She turned and trudged away from him, went to her room and sat on her bed. In time she arose, looked at her face in the mirror and suddenly was pounding the top of the dresser, eyes tightly shut to hide the madness she had seen but it would not go away and she slumped on the floor, shuddering and shuddering and shuddering at what she had almost done.

When Lois knocked on the door hours later to ask Karen if she had decided to miss dinner, as well as lunch, she found a composed young woman sitting on the edge of her bed putting pale pink polish on neatly shaped nails. Karen looked up with a smile.

'I'll be right there, Lois.'

The table she shared with Lois was near the end of the room, close to the buffet, and she walked unseeingly through the throngs of people to get there, only to hesitate, uncertain. The table was set for three, and Lois was not there yet. She startled when a hand touched her arm with impersonal politeness and a voice she remembered as an angry one, said suavely, 'Won't you sit down?'

Flicking a glance over her shoulder Karen saw a broad chest under a pale cream shirt open at the neck to reveal a deep mahogony tan. Looking further up as she slid into her seat, she was struck by the aliveness of this man; his craggy face, his beak-like nose, his sharp, dark eyes snapped and crackled with life as did his crisp shock of untidy dark hair. My God! she thought, lowering her gaze, he looks like an angry eagle!

He spun a chair out, sat on it across from her and gave her an intent, searching stare before saying, 'So this is what a coward looks like in one of her better moments!'

Karen blinked, frowned and said coolly, 'I beg your pardon?'

'You heard it. At first I thought you were just an ignorant tourist who didn't have sense enough to keep away from cliffs, but when I pulled you back and saw what was in your face, I wished I'd let you go.' He leaned forward as he spoke and Karen flinched back at the cool, amused contempt in his tone.

'You have no right . . .'

'I have every right! Whether you like it

or not, I saved your worthless neck, Mrs Jamison, and according to some customs, that means I own you. Not that I want to, of course, but there it is. Lois had already pointed you out to me as another unescorted guest and suggested I make myself friendly. I was about to do so when I saw you bent on ruining a new enterprise for Lois, and if it hadn't been for her, I may just have given you a shove after dragging you back. I sure don't want you around my neck!'

What she might have said in reply, had he given her a chance to reply, Karen was not to know, for at that moment he went off on a surprisingly new tack, saying, 'This is such a nice place, isn't it, Mrs Jamison? Or may I call you Karen? Lois has been a friend of the family since I was a child and . . . Oh, hi, Lois! I was just telling Mrs Jamison . . .'

'Yes, I heard you, Brent. What's the matter with you two? Why aren't you eating? Come on, Karen, you must be starved after missing lunch.' She seemed totally unaware of any atmosphere between her companions, and beamed when Brent got lithely to his feet, scooping up Karen's plate as well as his own.

'I'll get something for Karen, save her

the trip. You come with me and tell me what's good.'

When the two returned, laughing, with laden plates, Karen was still in a wordless state of shock. No one, but no one! had ever spoken to her like that! What right did that man have to call her a coward, to say that since he had saved her, she belonged to him, and then to say that he wished he hadn't bothered because he didn't want her dragging around his neck!

Lois kicked her gently under the table. 'Look,' she whispered, 'I know he's gorgeous, but don't stare; he'll get a swelled head!' Gorgeous! Him!

The man turned from the couple to whom he'd been talking and smiled pleasantly at Karen. 'I'm sorry, I should have asked. Don't you like shrimp salad?' He looked genuinely concerned! How could anyone be so two-faced?

'She loves it, Brent,' gurgled Lois happily. 'Says she could never have too much of it. Come on, Karen love, eat up. Don't make a liar of me!'

Forcing a smile at her hostess Karen put a mouthful of shrimp salad into herself and tried to swallow, knowing she was going to choke. Surprisingly, it slid down quite easily as did the next and the next and

26

then a bite of baked potato with sour cream, some of the crisp green salad, the roast beef, the crusty roll, a sip of wine and bite after bite until there were only scraps left on her plate and the man, Brent who had been insidiously charming throughout the meal was returning with apple pie, cheese and coffee.

Lois pushed her cup away and smiled benignly at the other two. 'Well,' she said, self-satisfied, 'I'm so glad you came, Brent. This hasn't been much fun for Karen so far; she doesn't like being a third wheel. Now that there's two of you singles you can join forces and be partners for dancing, tennis, cards . . . all sorts of things!'

'Oh, indeed,' said Brent smoothly, 'all sorts of things.'

'I'm sure your friend can amuse himself,' said Karen stiffly, 'and equally sure he doesn't want me slung around his neck gratuitously. I'll say goodnight, now.'

She was stopped dead by a heavy hand on her shoulder, a hand which may have looked, to an observer, to be gentle, but which hurt! 'Oh, no,' he said with dangerous politeness and an evil glint in his pewter eyes, 'you can't do that. We must have a nice walk to help us digest our meal

27

so we can dance the evening away. Right, Lois?'

'Right, Brent. Oh, yes!'

'See? I'll give you exactly six minutes to do whatever you need to do and put on a jacket and if you're not back here by then I'll bust your door down,' he said jocularly with deadly seriousness, 'and then I'll have to pay damages to Lois.'

As she left, Karen heard Lois laugh delightedly and say, 'The door you can have for free, Brent . . .'

In four minutes she was walking rapidly up the path to the seclusion of the forest when a hand on her elbow and a voice stopped her saying, 'A slow walk's much better for the digestion, coward.'

TWO

'I'm not a coward!' Karen wrenched herself out of his grasp and ran toward the trees, hoping to lose herself, seeking a place to hide, needing to escape, but he kept pace with her easily, never giving her a moment's respite, never letting up on the mocking, amused speech he seemed intent on making.

'You must be, you're still running away, just like you tried to do this morning on the cliff. I told you you belong to me now and I'm not going to let you keep on running from whatever it is you're trying to escape. What's the matter, Karen, why are you still running?'

At that moment Karen ceased running; she tripped on a root and fell to her knees, giving the man Brent time to pounce, to drag her into a sitting position and sit beside her, holding her down with one long arm pinned across her shoulders.

'There, now!' he said as if she had sat by him voluntarily. 'That's better. Much friendlier! Who can carry on a proper conversation at twenty-five miles an hour? You're Mrs Jamison; where's Mister?'

'He's dead.'

For once the mockery left his face, and in the dim light cast by the moon Karen could see a look of consternation twist his features momentarily. 'Oh.' The word fell between them flatly. 'Sorry, Karen. Recently?'

She was forced by something in her to tell the truth, 'Three and a half years ago,' and the mockery was back, as she had known it would be.

'That's carrying self-pity a bit far, isn't it? If you'd been going to do the cowardly thing, you should have done it ages ago!'

'Will you quit calling me a coward!' she all but screamed at him. 'What difference does it make to you what I am, what I do?'

'No difference at all except that Lois is a friend of mine and she's just started out here hoping to make a life for herself after hers has been torn apart by a thoughtless husband and an ungrateful son. Her husband of thirty years died ten months ago and left the farm to her son, with the understanding, but nothing on paper, that he would provide for his mother, give her a home as long as she needed it. He wouldn't. He allowed his wife to make Lois feel unwelcome in her own home, and treated his young sister like dirt. Lois left, made a down payment on this place with what she had actually been left by her husband, got a mortgage for the rest and is trying hard.

'But you don't see her going around with a long face; she's too busy. You don't find her running away from life, interfering with other people to the extent that you've interfered with me, do you?'

'I'm not interfering with you! You're interfering with me!'

'Only because you forced me into it, forced me to save your scrawny little neck. If I had let you go, can't you just see the headlines? YOUNG WOMAN THROWS HERSELF FROM CLIFF AT HOLIDAY RESORT. Or, even worse, GUEST AT RESORT FALLS OVER DANGEROUS CLIFF. What do you think would happen to her chances of making good then?'

'I wasn't really going to do it, damn you! I was just so lonely, and that loneliness was pointed up so sharply by everyone else here having someone of their own and it was too much! But I wasn't going to do it!'

'Yes you were!' He shot the words at her,

31

angry. 'So you're lonely! Hell, everyone's lonely! You're lonely, Lois is lonely! Thousands of people are lonely! So don't go making any bids for sympathy to me, because you won't get it. Your husband's been gone for a long time and it's time you grew up and quit going around looking like a tragedy queen, hoping everyone'll tut-tut and tiptoe around in the presence of your grief. If you want me to believe you're not a coward, that you wouldn't have gone over the edge, you'll drag yourself up out of the dirt and put on a pretty dress and dance the evening away so Lois can quit worrying about you!'

'No! I can't!' she cried agitatedly. 'You don't know all . . .'

'And I don't want to!' He hauled her to her feet, shoving her ahead of him down the path. 'All I want is for Lois to have some peace of mind about you. You owe her that much, don't you think?'

'Why? I'm paying my own way! She's been kind, more than kind, but I don't see that I owe her more than a debt of gratitude for asking me to share her table and some of her evenings!'

'You, my dear Mrs Jamison, are occupying the room her daughter was in until she sent her to stay with friends to make room for you. And her daughter is just about her only solace!'

'I didn't know! I didn't!' walled Karen.

'Then how d'you think you got a room at such short notice? People have to book three months in advance . . . at the very least!'

'I . . . wasn't well,' she replied lamely. 'All the arrangements were made for me and I just accepted them.' Why was it that everything she said to him sounded like she was whining?

'Of course,' he jeered. 'Cowards always just accept; never think or do for themselves.'

'I told you not to call me that!'

'Then prove I'm wrong. Come and dance and start acting like a big girl for a change!'

Karen went back, her head held high for the first time in months, her pert nose sticking up in the air, her shoulders squared, an angry ring to her heels on the flagstones of the path. She was totally unaware of the gradual relaxation of the craggy, stern face of the man behind her, of the softening in his eyes which changed from pewter almost to turquoise and of the amused smile which twitched at his mouth as she stalked into her room to change into something suitable for dancing.

She stood staring into her nearly empty closet and for the first time in years was forced to face the fact of her sadly depleted wardrobe. Like many women before her, the thought flashed through her mind: I haven't a thing to wear! And unlike many, in her case it was absolutely true!

There were two cotton skirts, one badly in need of an iron, the other with part of the hem down. Beside them hung three pairs of slacks, all too large for her because she had lost weight since buying them, a pair of jeans which fit quite well but that she had intended to wash the next day, some shorts, blouses and tee-shirts. With trembling hands she riffled through the poor collection and then angrily slammed the door to the closet, causing the waiting man outside her room to wince. She picked up her brush, tore it through her hair, grabbed a fistful of pins and bundled its pale glory into a bun on top of her head, the way she wore it under her cap. A few swift, angry swoops with a mascara wand, a touch of shadow and a smear of lipstick and she shoved her feet into sandals, clicked off the light and marched from the room. Her eyes were bright with anger and her chin was still high. HE was waiting for her!

'Well,' Karen snarled, 'here I am. Take me as you find me or not at all. I don't own a dress!'

He flicked a hooded, sardonic glance up and down her figure and said coolly, 'That thing's nice enough. It'll do.'

'That thing' was a navy-blue jump suit with white piping around the scooped neckline and cuffs of the short sleeves. It was a little too big for her and a bit short with the sandals she was wearing but Karen couldn't have cared less. All that mattered now was holding onto the delicious feeling of anger which was coursing through her veins, giving her a reason to live. All she knew was that she was no longer in an emotional void, that at last she was feeling and she let it build, let it carry her along with its thundering force. God! it was good to be feeling!

He swung her onto the floor and proceeded to gyrate in front of her in a manner she did not recognize and she stayed utterly still, eyeing him coldly until the beat of the music, the motion of his sinuous body, the mockery in his cold, hard eyes started her moving, tentatively, clumsily, then with more and more grace until she was dancing along with the crowd, almost unaware of them, but never, never, unaware of her partner and when the music changed tempo, became slow and sensuous, he drew her against him and she shuddered, stiffened, stumbling frequently as they danced.

They circled the floor, once, twice, a third time, his arm loose around her, his head erect and somehow aloof. She sneaked a glance at his face.

He was staring across the room into nothingness, an expression of deep sadness on his countenance and unbidden, the words he had spoken at the edge of the forest intruded into her mind: 'Hell! Everyone's lonely!' Was he? And sad along with it? And if he were, why couldn't he respect her feelings and leave her alone as she wanted him to? What business of his was it whether she lived or died, other, of course, than his concern for Lois Granger and her new enterprise! Unconsciously Karen sighed and was immediately turned from the floor to a table on the patio.

She sat in sullen silence until he put a tall drink in front of her and seated himself. Karen glared at him with pure loathing. 'I didn't ask for a drink.'

'You've got one. Smile, Lois is watching.'

Karen bared her even white teeth while her eyes never lost their icy gleam. 'Now I suppose we have to chat happily?' she snapped.

'Of course. Just as we danced so well together.'

'But we didn't! At first I didn't have a clue what you were doing, bouncing around like an idiot!'

'You picked it up quick enough,' he observed. 'Everyone dances like that nowadays. It's not my fault you haven't been dancing in so long that you don't know how, so why look at me as if it is?'

'I wasn't!' she grated at him, still with her teeth bared in a travesty of a smile while her eyes threw messages of malevolence at him. 'And you can't say you enjoyed the waltz with me because I looked at you and you were miserable!'

'We all have our little problems,' he said pleasantly, and she wanted to choke him, 'I was thinking about someone I care for a great deal who longs to be able to dance and can't, and there I was with someone who was hating every minute of it, not one whit grateful for strong legs to carry her while music wove magic ribbons of sound. Oh,' he added at her raised brows, 'not my words, hers.'

'Who is she?' Karen was compelled to ask.

'Just a girl, one of many. Like most people, you wouldn't care about her or the others.'

'She's crippled, I take it.'

'Only physically,' he said pointedly, sipped from his drink, lit a cigarette.

'You obviously care.' The only way to deal with him was to ignore his inuendo . . . 'Why aren't you with her, doing something about it?'

'In my own way, I am doing something about it. When are you going to do something about your own crippling affliction?'

'I'm not crippled!' she snapped, forgetting to smile, or at least pretend to.

'Of course you are!' He actually laughed aloud. 'You shuddered when I put my arm around you to dance. If you can't stand having a man touch you even so impersonally as during a dance, then you're an emotional cripple. What do you do for a living, anyway? Keep a light-house?'

'I'm an R.N., and if I shuddered when you touched me it's only because I can't stand *you*, not because I can't stand men!'

'Really? Then how come you haven't had a date in so long you've forgotten how to dance and have never learned the newer ones?'

'I simply did not want to!'

'Didn't want to, or weren't asked?' he sneered.

Karen leapt to her feet. 'I don't have to take this from you!' She spun to leave but he was with her in one lithe movement, slipping her into his arms as if they had both risen to dance.

'Stop struggling,' he whispered into her ear, and to Lois, watching, it appeared he might be whispering something entirely different. She smiled happily to herself and went off to her own quarters.

'God!' he was whispering in her ear, his hot breath torturing her, 'how I pity your poor patients. I wonder if it hurts you as much to touch them as it does to touch me?'

'Of course not! I loved my patients!'

'Loved?'

'Love!' she insisted, but it was too late. His steel-trap mind had clamped on her one wrong word.

'Oh no! You said "loved", and "loved" you meant. Past tense, Karen. You quit?' When she made no reply, only struggled against his hold, her breath coming in harsh rasps, he took it to the next logical step. 'What's the matter, get fired for being such a cold fish?'

This was beyond endurance! She swung a fist and clouted him across the side of the face. 'Mind your own damned business!' she screamed, and tore out of the room, leaving a crowd of gawking, smirking strangers staring first after her, then at the hard, craggy face of the man who returned their stares expressionlessly and strode away.

Karen stayed in her room the next morning until she was sure that a man's natural hunger would have driven Brent to eat, and his own natural animal aliveness driven him out and into some activity before she ventured forth. He wasn't around, so she quickly gulped coffee and slipped from the hotel to hide in what she had come to think of as her own private cove.

It was reached by a set of steep, ladder-like stairs which clung to the cliff-side until the narrow strip of gravel was spread out at the bottom, with one large, flat rock for sitting, and china hats, chitons, periwinkles, tiny, scuttling hermit crabs carrying their houses with them and, at low tide, as it was now, a thousand fat purple starfish lining the walls of the cove. Karen delighted in the place. In the suck and surge of the water which creamed around the base of the rock, tickled and teased the starfish, rolled the hermits about and washed the periwinkles, giving them a damp sheen, she found a form of timelessness, a sort of peace which was balm to her spirits.

In a small tidal pool lived a few inch-long bullheads which darted and dashed from shadow to shadow, visible only when in motion. She sat now, shading her eyes the better to see, and dropped pieces of crushed periwinkle into the water to encourage the diminutive fish out of seclusion.

A crushing footstep in the gravel behind her caused her to start and turn abruptly. 'Ouch!' she yelped, hand flying to a neck muscle as the sudden stab of pain up into the top of her head brought tears to her eyes. 'You startled me!' she said accusingly to the man who was right beside her.

'Oh, poor girl,' said Ralph Hodges. 'And you kinked your neck. Here, let me rub it for you. Lisa says I have magic hands . . .' Without waiting for a reply he hunkered beside her and pushed her hand aside, kneading the knotted muscle, talking all the while. 'You're a very beautiful woman,

Karen, and many times I've wanted to ask you to join us, but Lisa said you'd be uncomfortable . . . an odd woman at a table with three couples. We're with my brother and his wife, and her sister and her husband, so we're sort of a family party. You're a divorcée, I heard someone say . . . you must be lonely . . .' While he talked his fingers kept circling the lumpy muscle in her neck, strongly, and then more and more sensuously until she tried to pull away, realizing what he was up to.

'That's enough, thanks,' she said briskly, trying to get to her feet, but the hand remained on the soft skin at the nape of her neck, caressing openly now while his other hand kept pressure on her shoulder, holding her down. 'I said that's enough!' Karen spoke sharply. 'Stop it!'

'Aaah . . . no,' he crooned breathily, still rubbing his fingers on her neck, still holding her tightly while the massage went slowly up into her hair then trailed out again, in soft, insinuating, circling strokes. 'You like it . . . I like it . . . Your hair's like corn-silk, your skin's like a baby's.'

Karen jerked her head back, catching him on the point of his chin and jumped to her feet when he inadvertently let go of her to rub his own injury. But quickly he was on his feet, his arms pinning her to his panting chest, his hand on her cheek, forcing her face around and she grasped it with both of her own, pulling it around to bite it, and at the same time saying loudly, 'No!' He caught her hands, pinned both of them behind her back and laughed softly, triumphantly. 'I love it when you struggle . . . you're rubbing your body . . .'

He broke off when a sharp voice called out, 'Ralph!', and dropped Karen like a hot potato, turning, as a brick-red flush stole up his face and he said, 'Oh, hi, honey. The lady got a kink in her neck and I was trying to fix it the way I do yours. Poor girl, I startled her and she jumped. What kept you, anyway? You said you'd be here right away!'

The question and last statement were fired at the woman rapidly, almost accusingly, and she blinked once or twice before saying defensively, 'I was talking to Jane and Harv. I wasn't all that far behind you! But some people, it seems,' she shot Karen a malicious look, 'work pretty damned fast!'

'Now wait a minute!' Karen wasn't about to take that kind of insinuation from anyone! 'I did not want your husband's help, he insisted on offering it!'

'Oh, sure, I'll just bet! I know my Ralph! He's so darned shy I practically had to propose to him myself, so I know who instigated this little episode. You divorcées! Just because you can't hold your own man, you think anyone's husband's fair game! Well let me tell you . . .'

What else she might have told Karen was lost in the triumphant, and unexpected, shout: 'Hey, Karen! I found one!' And into the little bay came Brent, perched in the bow of a tiny skiff, paddling with one oar, smiling, ignoring the other two. 'Come on, get in and I'll show you!' The bow of the boat bumped the flat rock and he practically dragged Karen in, dumping her bodily on the centre seat, shoving the oar into her hand, pushing the other one into the lock, saying, 'You row again, I'll direct you. Sorry, you two,' to the silent couple on the rock, 'no room. My girl and I are going to see a petroglyph.'

'Row, dammit!' he hissed at Karen as he pushed the boat off and sat in the stern.

She rowed.

'Go back the way I came,' he said quietly and she obediently turned the small craft and pointed it into the next little bight until they were out of sight of the bay where she had just been sitting. 'O.K., stop,' he told her gently and she dropped the oars, letting them dangle loosely while reaction overcame her in the form of violent trembling.

'What was that all about?' he asked when she was somewhat recovered and puffing jerkily on the cigarette he had passed her.

She explained as best she could but then said, 'You . . . I mean . . . how . . . why?'

'I heard you holler "No!" and turned the boat to head this way, then heard the other woman call out, "Ralph!", and being the inveterate eavesdropper I am, kept out of sight to see what developed. When she attacked you, instead of her husband, whom I knew should have been the one under attack, I decided to put a stop to it the best way I knew how. If she's afraid of you because you don't have a man of your own, the best thing to do was give you one. Right?'

He grinned charmingly and in spite of herself, Karen found herself smiling shakily. 'But I slugged you last night!'

'Damn right! And maybe I deserved it,' he admitted surprisingly, then spoiled it all by saying musingly, 'Lois doesn't need this kind of trouble, either! And don't think a jealous woman can't make a lot of it!' He looked at her consideringly for a moment or two. 'We could still have problems with that girl and her husband, so why not keep up the pretence of friendship just to keep them both in line?'

'For Lois's sake?' Why did she feel hurt?

'Of course for Lois's sake! Friends, then?' He fixed her with his eagle-stare, eyes dark grey and probing.

'O.K. . . . friends. But I don't even know what your last name is . . . or what a petroglyph is!'

'As to the first, it's Cookson. And for the second, I really did find one. Want to see?

'It was carved maybe two thousand years ago, and some put it as far back as four thousand. See?' Brent ran his finger along the outline of the figure gouged out of the solid rock wall of the inlet. 'I'm told this represents a bear, symbol of ferocity and strength to the Indians who owned this land before our forefathers took it and civilization swept them out of its way.' He held the boat in close to the shore while Karen traced the two wide circles which must surely represent eyes, the curving lines meant to indicate ears, the wide, snarling mouth and the taloned front paws alongside. It was carved, maybe half an inch deep and stood half in the water, half out, two and a half feet from top to bottom.

'But they must have worked only at low tide,' she said, 'and even then part of their carving would have been done under water. This must have taken years to do! Look how intricate it is, and to think they could only work on it when the water was down!'

'That may be . . . or may not. No one's sure. The water level may have been much lower when this was done, especially if it is four thousand years old . . .' His voice trailed off. He was thinking, as was Karen, of the vastness of time, and of how insignificant one small human life is in the whole scheme of earth.

'I wonder if he knew . . . suspected, when he was doing this work, that it would endure?' said Karen at length. 'I watched so many of my patients die and as their remains were taken away, there seemed to be nothing left, no artifacts, no reminders that they had ever existed. Is that what we've become, nonentities who are born, live and die, leaving nothing behind as this man did? Oh, I don't mean we should all carve our initials on rocks and trees, but there must be more to life than what each of us . . . the modern ones . . . are leaving.' Her voice quavered slightly and she swallowed, turning her head aside, ashamed of being what he might call 'self-pitying', again.

'How do you know we aren't leaving something?' he asked quietly, and didn't seem patronizing or sneering at all! 'We may be doing things unaware, as did this fellow, here. I don't believe he thought about distant generations seeing his art and wondering; I think all he was doing was appeasing his gods in his own way, or worshipping, or trying to gain the strength of the bear by making his image in the stone. Who are we to know that a chance word of ours might not change the outlook of one other human, and in changing the outlook, change the life just that one, tiny amount, so that things happen in this way, instead of that. You might see an angry youth on a street corner, a boy with a grudge against the world, a boy intending to rob a bank or commit another crime, and you smile at him, say "Good morning," and he blinks, takes another look around and says, "Hey, that nurse smiled at me! Nurses must be pretty nice people." And from that moment on, things change for him. He grows, matures, becomes a famous surgeon, saves a life that might otherwise have been lost and the life he saves becomes a great artist, or statesman or writer who leaves a mark on the rocks of time for future generations to point to. And all because you smiled at a boy.'

Karen gulped, tried to smile, but found her mouth twisted by a sadness she couldn't control. How many things weren't now going to happen because she had spent so much time hiding from the world, keeping herself from becoming involved?

'Hey! Don't be sad,' he said. 'That was only a very poor illustration of how each of us may be instrumental in the forming of society. It wasn't to be taken as a basis for daily living! That has to be done minute by minute, without thought being given to each little act of ours. The fact that we might change things is only to be borne if we do it unconsciously. Come on, friend, smile!'

Karen smiled, suddenly light-hearted . . . or was it light-headed? . . . and pushed the boat away from the ancient petroglyph. 'Talking to four-thousand year old ghosts makes me hungry,' she cried, taking the oars and rowing madly toward the dock in front of the hotel. 'If you're responsible for me, and by your own choice, you say you are, it's up to you to keep me fed!'

Brent laughed and scooped up a handful of water, splashing her. 'You bet, lady! It'd be a bit redundant if I had saved your neck just to let you starve!'

'My worthless neck,' she reminded him.

'Maybe not,' he admitted, his eyes laughing into hers. 'Who knows, you might smile at a boy and . . .'

Karen stuck her tongue out at him and said, 'Uh-uh! I reserve that for married men! Us divorcées, you know . . .'

The smile they shared as the boat floated into the wharf and bumped gently was one of complete understanding and the beginnings of something more.

THREE

Within the space of a week Karen and Brent had become a recognized couple in this small world of nothing but, and as such were invited to join many group outings, activities, card parties and tournaments, both on the golf course, where Karen did not shine, but Brent did, and on the tennis courts where they were just about equal. But their favourite pastime was to wonder along the shore, beachcombing, swimming now and then and talking, always talking.

But, though they talked of many subjects, feeling their way around each other's personalities, learning likes and dislikes, the talk never became very personal, Karen shying off if he became too probing, or, on the other hand, too open about himself. She was not yet ready for that. Keep it light, keep it gay, seemed to be the attitude she could best cope with and Brent was quite content to let her set the pace.

Except for one lazy, sunny afternoon . . .

They were sprawled on a big air mattress on the gravel of the little cove where

Ralph had accosted Karen, and this was the subject of their conversation. 'He keeps looking at me funny,' said Karen. 'Not funny-amusing, but funny-odd. As if he's afraid or uncomfortable or something.'

'Probably wondering just what he'd have done if you'd taken him up on his pass, or if his wife hadn't come along just when she did and he'd been forced to carry it through. You shouldn't have struggled, Karen. He'd probably have been so darned scared he'd have taken off screaming!'

She giggled. 'What a way to parry a pass! Scare the guy off by accepting? Where'd I have been if I'd tried that and he'd accepted?'

'In a skiff, out in mid-channel before you could have gone one step further!'

'Huh! You didn't even know I was there until you heard me squawk!' Karen rolled over onto her stomach and reached for a peach from the bag in front of her. Brent stayed her hand, took the peach, bit enormously and handed it back, juice running off his chin.

'No? That's what I told you. You believe everything you're told?'

'I believe your mother should have taught you to use a napkin,' she grinned.

'There's juice all over your mouth . . . on your chin, too.'

'Get rid of it for me,' he said, his face coming close, blocking out the sun, his eyes laughing down into hers. He was flirting again as he had done now and then and she wished he wouldn't do it! It reminded her of the day they had gone to the head of the inlet to have a picnic, just the two of them, beside the roar and spray of Chatterbox Falls . . .

They had swum for a long time in the cold water of the pool at the base of the falls and then had eaten their lunch in a sort of numbed silence, both aware of the jolt of electricity that had coursed between them when they had accidently brushed almost naked bodies together. It was early in their first week of friendship and had sobered Karen to a great extent, making her think, wonder, and when they had both finished eating, she had gathered up the trash and taken it to burn in the big drum at the edge of the pool, leaving him reclining indolently against a tree, his long legs stretched out in the grass.

'Tidy by nature, aren't you?' he asked, half-opening his eyes, chewing on a stem of grass.

'I suppose so, why?'

'No reason. Just that you seem to like to have everything in it's place, all neatly tied up.'

'That's so bad?' Karen crushed the egg-shells with a stick, dropped it into the fire and averted her face as he got to his feet, strolled toward her.

'I didn't say it was bad,' he smiled. 'just odd, I guess. I wonder what you'd do if I kissed you now that we're both fully clothed and not in a pool of water with the falls thundering in our ears?' When she made to move away, he laughed, his eyes dancing. 'Oh, I know what went through your head when I came up underneath you; you panicked, thinking I was going to try to make love to you and we didn't even know one another well! That's what I mean, everything in its place, everything in its neat little time slot.'

'We *don't* know one another well!' she had protested indignantly. 'And I didn't want you to kiss me then. I don't want you to kiss me now!'

'All right,' he said lightly. 'I won't . . . if you're sure . . . ? And his laughing eyes mocked her when it took her a long time, *too* long a time to answer:

'I'm sure!'

'Karen!' She pulled herself back from that far time and place to see that he was still leaning close to her and that the laughter had died from his eyes. He didn't look at all like he was flirting, this time!

'The peach juice . . .' Had his voice ever been that soft?

'I don't have a napkin,' Karen replied, her eyes held captive by his. A catch in her throat made it hard to breathe.

'Don't you like peach juice?' he whispered. She continued to stare at him wordlessly, unable to retreat, and just as unable to advance. 'Or don't you like me?' The words were hardly more than a sigh.

'I like you . . .' Her heart began to thunder in its frail cage, threatening to escape. Her eyelids grew heavy, her breath came in slow, painful lungfuls. She knew she was going to kiss him, did not want to, ached to, longed to, afraid, but was compelled to reach her mouth up to his which was waiting so confidently. 'I . . . Brent . . .' she said, shaking her head. 'Oh, don't make me . . .'

'Don't make you make the first move?' he breathed against her lips just in the instant before he claimed them as his warm hands on her shoulders turned her onto her back. Without her knowing how it happened her arms were around him, her mouth opening to the demands of his and her breasts were crushed under his weight until she thought she would die from the pain, the exquisite agony of the pressure of him touching every inch of her, making her throat ache with tears which spurted forth from her eyes. His lips left hers to travel up her face and into her hair, back to her mouth, her throat, her seeking lips, again and again.

He turned on his side, still holding her locked tightly to him, cradling her shaking, sobbing body close as he whispered, 'No, no, Karen. Stop now. It's all right . . . There, now, don't . . .'

'Oh . . . Marty!' she moaned and he let her go then, let her pull herself away from him, wrapped her in her big towel and kept quiet for a few moments. He stood her on her feet then and gently propelled her toward the steps and up the cliff-side. From far away came the sound of an outboard whining against the tide, a gull crying, the water lapping at the rocks and her own voice, choked, apologizing brokenly.

'I understand, Karen. Truly I do!' he assured her, but she knew it was not true.

How could Brent understand what she hardly understood herself? She couldn't accept this wild passion which had taken her in its thrall the moment his lips touched hers! Not only was there the feeling of guilt, of disloyalty to an old memory, but the terrible knowledge that never, not once, had she responded to Marty like that! She had loved him, wanted him, but never had he made her blood sing the way Brent just had, never had he turned her into the quivering, demanding piece of flesh and bone and she felt horribly, deeply ashamed of herself. She wanted to run, to hide, from the entire world, but most of all from this man who had triggered the latent streak of wantonness that was in her.

At the top of the cliff when she tried to turn toward the hotel he drew her in the opposite direction. Karen pulled away sharply. 'No!' she gasped.

'Karen.' Brent spoke firmly. 'I'm not going to try to seduce you, for pete's sake! You're in no shape to put in a public appearance. Come over here into the shade and sit down for a bit, until you're calmer. I'm going back down to the beach for the mattress and things.' He eased her into a sitting position, forced her to face him. 'Stay here. Promise me you'll wait right here!'

Karen nodded, more to get rid of him than anything, but while he was gone, although she wanted to flee, she was kept pinned to her position by a strange lethargy as well as the certain knowledge that if she did leave, he would search her out.

When he returned, mattress folded under one arm, towel bundled under the other, and bag of fruit dangling from one fist, he gave her a watchful glance then sat by her, not touching, but somehow his presence was . . . warming.

He took a few huckleberries from a bush and tossed them, one by one, high into the air, catching them in his mouth, completely relaxed. A bird trilled liquidly and Brent said, 'Let's talk.'

'There's nothing to talk about.'

'Of course there is. We shared a pretty steamy embrace, a few kisses, and on the basis of that you fell apart with guilt . . . guilt, which I might add, while probably quite normal, is just a little bit delayed. If you were going to feel guilty about kissing another man after you lost your husband, you should have done it years ago, the first time it happened.'

She was unable to reply. How could she say to him now: 'That was the first.' She couldn't! He turned her face toward his with a finger on her chin, looked smilingly into her eyes. 'So what's the big storm all about, hmm?'

Her eyes dropped and he let her chin go, a speculative look on his face when she said, 'No reason, I guess. I'm sorry. It won't happen again.'

He chuckled. 'Meaning I'm going to get a chance to kiss you like that again?' But he made no attempt to do so, only took her left hand in his and rubbed his thumb over her wedding band. 'Think you'd feel better without that?'

Karen shook her head. 'Tell me about him.' Brent said quietly. 'What line was he in?'

'He was a policeman.' What more was there to say about Martin Jamison? He lived and breathed for his job. From earliest childhood that had been all he wanted to be. He and Karen had grown up together and when he was a rookie she had gone to the mainland to nursing school, partly because she had always wanted to be a nurse, but mainly to be near Marty. They had known since she was ten and he twelve that they were going to marry one day . . .

'How long did you have together, Karen?'

'All our lives,' she replied. 'Typical boy and girl next door story, but we only had three months together, married. The night after my graduation he was coming home from the boys' club he supervised and a drunk ran his car up on the sidewalk, pinning Marty to a building. He lived for six hours and was conscious for two of them. He was in such pain!'

The agony she still felt at the memory of her husband's pain was reflected in her face, echoed in her voice, and Brent pulled her face down to his chest, patting her comfortingly.

'It's over now, Karen,' he said firmly. 'Do you think that knowing you were going to relive this every day would have made it easier for him to bear? Now snap out of it!'

She pulled away from him, accusing, doe-like eyes flying to his harsh face. 'Of course not!' she cried. 'But I can't stop reliving it. I don't want to keep on remembering, but I can't help it! How can you just say "stop"? Don't you have any compassion in your soul?'

'Sure,' he said easily, 'lots of it, but why waste pity on someone who has so much of it for herself that she doesn't need any more? What you should have done was gone back to work right away, buried your-

60

self in the problems and needs of your patients until there was no room for your own troubles.'

'I did! I was back at work two days after the funeral!'

'Yet you told me you had only been working for six months before you had to quit and come here for a rest . . . on your doctor's orders!' There was that note of scathing contempt again!

'I had to quit,' she told him heavily, 'a few months after Marty died.' But she couldn't go on, couldn't tell him why; he'd only accuse her of looking for sympathy again, so what was the point?

'Just like you had to quit a couple of weeks ago? Sure, work a few months and then fall apart, it's good for the soul and keeps everyone aware that you suffered a lot. Must be nice to have been left so well off that you can drop out just whenever the mood strikes. But you were saying you needed a job when this little break's over. Thought much about what you're going to do?'

'A little. Not that it's any of your business, but I'll find something . . .' 'To have been left so well off . . .' the words echoed madly through her mind while she thought of the terror she had felt watching the insurance money disappear in great, gulping bites, knowing that the tiny pension would never in a million years be enough . . .

'You said you couldn't go back to the old-folks' place where the only release for the patients was death; you don't want to work in an active hospital, the work is too hard,' he sneered, 'so that doesn't leave an R.N. too much choice, does it?'

'There's always private duty,' she claimed, striving to inject a positive note into her tone when all she could feel were increasing doubts.

He nodded. 'A highly paid personal maid, not good enough to be family, not lowly enough to be a servant, sort of sandwiched in between. Must be an exciting life . . . interesting, too. What's your next alternative?'

'Who says there has to be one? Give me a cigarette . . . please.'

'You smoke too much,' he admonished, but gave her one. '*I* say there has to be an alternative! Private duty to some fat, arthritic old matron just isn't your bag, kid.'

'There're other kinds of cases!'

'In these days, unless the patient's so darned sick that medicare simply can't avoid providing a private nurse, that's about the only patient you'll get who's rich enough to afford you. And if you were specialling a very sick one, it would likely be private duty within a hospital room, so there you go, one or the other.'

'I wouldn't like private duty in a hospital but if that were all there was, I'd have to ri . . . try it. What difference does it make to you, anyway?'

'Not much . . . oops! There's the dinner-gong. Come on, lazy, race you!'

He let her hold the lead until the last ten yards and then he leapt ahead to catch her as she flew, hair streaming, toward the steps, swinging her high in a wide circle and setting her on her feet in the curve of his arm, laughing down at her. 'There's one more alternative we'll scratch: No sick old men! You'd never outrun 'em!'

In spite of her annoyance at his interfering ways, Karen had to admit his charm and laughed back up at him, thinking, In a way, it's nice to have someone interfere, someone to care about what I do with my life . . . He dropped a friendly kiss on her nose, one on her curved mouth, and said, 'You just enjoy the next few days, Karen-mine. There's one more alternative we'll have to discuss, but not until just before we leave here. Let's go. I'm starving!'

That night Karen lay awake for hours watching the pattern of moonlight through the branches of the tree just outside her window. He had called her that! He had said 'Karen-mine'. Was it just a figure of speech, as loosely used as 'honey' or 'sweetheart'? He had never called her either of the other two, had only flirted casually now and then until today, so there was no valid reason for this warmth in her face, all over her body, for the way her heart pounded and her chest ached as if she weren't getting enough oxygen. There was just no reason for it all! But still she tossed and turned, filled with a burning longing she could not suppress, hugging to herself the knowledge that in the morning she would be with him . . .

When she got to the breakfast table it was to hear that Brent had gone with a group of other men to a lake far back in the hills on a trout-fishing expedition. The emptiness of her day without Brent shocked her and she cleaned her room thoroughly, although guests were expected to make their own beds and dust, asked Lois for more to do, used the big mangle to iron sheets and pillow cases, sorted the records for the dance that evening and afterwards played doubles with some other women who had been abandoned for elusive trout.

After the furious sets she had played, Karen slumped in a deck chair and accepted with a smile the glass of iced tea Gwen, one of her fellow guests, handed her. Gwen, short, plumpish, with a mass of yellow curls, was vivacious and popular with everyone. 'Hey,' she said, bubbling as she normally did, 'there's supposed to be a pretty good waterfall to visit down the inlet a bit. A bunch of us are taking some of the outboards tomorrow and wondered if you and Brent would like to come along.'

Karen smiled. 'Sure! As far as I'm concerned, anyway. I'd love it. But I can't speak for Brent of course.'

Gwen looked uncomfortable. 'I . . . hope he'll want to join us . . . you see, it's only couples going and . . . well . . . you wouldn't enjoy yourself in the midst of us married folks . . . would you?' Her green eyes looked slightly sick as they slid away from Karen's.

'No. I probably wouldn't.' Karen's voice was flat, dull, as she got to her feet, stung by the knowledge that only as an appendage of Brent was she welcome. Just like it had been before he came on the scene, Karen, alone, was simply not wanted. 'I'll pass then. Thanks anyway Gwen.'

Gwen, knowing that the other woman was hurt, tried to make amends as Karen departed, saying she had to wash her hair. 'Oh, let me! I'd love to, really I would!'

'No thanks. I'm used to doing things for myself.'

The fishermen returned late in the day, tired, hungry and dirty. Karen's heart lightened as she returned Brent's warm smile across the room as he headed hurriedly toward the bath. During the evening she found, to her dismay, that he wanted to re-hash the day's fishing with the men who had accompanied him, and Karen, wanting to avoid being asked in his presence to join in the expedition to the waterfall, had necessarily to avoid him! She sat talking to Lois for some time until he came across to drag her away. The music had started.

'We're going down the inlet tomorrow,' he told her, 'to see a waterfall.'

'Thank you, but I'm not,' she said, trying not to look sulky, and afraid that she was failing miserably. He just looked askance at her, saying no more about it. Later, she saw him talking to Gwen, shaking his head, looking over at her, and in one of those sudden silences which sometimes comes over a noisy group, the girl's voice rang out loud and clear, with her tinkling laugh preceding it:

'Oh, but that doesn't mean you have to miss it! An extra man's always welcome! Please come, Brent.' She tucked her little, dimpled hand into the crook of his arm and smiled up at him, all charm, all eager girl. Karen left the room.

Brent came to her later when she was feeling chilled from having sat outside on a wall for too long, and they danced for a while. But it was no good; the evening was spoiled for Karen and she went off to bed feeling much different from the night before. Brent, as far as she knew, stayed in the warm, bright lounge and enjoyed himself immensely.

She was small-minded enough to feel pleased when she awoke to a stormy morning and knew that the proposed trip down the inlet would have to be abandoned. She lay in her bed for a long time listening to the hollow bong, bong, bong, of an oil drum beating itself to death on the rocks, and when she arose, sat on her window-sill to watch the endless rows of grey, white-capped waves pour inexorably by.

The dining room, when she eventually stirred herself enough to go there, was filled with gloomy, glowering faces and low, disgruntled conversation. The only bright spot, to Karen's eyes, was Brent, waiting with ill-concealed impatience for her to join him. 'Come on! The trout'll be all gone,' he claimed, towing her to the buffet and loading his plate, urging her to do the same.

'I just want toast and coffee,' she protested. 'Leave the trout for the men who caught them.'

'In case you haven't noticed, I'm a man and I caught ten of these beauties. If I want to give you three of them, then you'll accept them with good grace.' He slapped them on her plate, added fried potatoes and eggs before her goggling eyes.

'I can't eat all that!'

'You'd better, my girl. I want you well fed. That last alternative I mentioned is going to require a lot of strength!' He positively *leered* at her! And in that moment, a smouldering spark inside her burst into a flicker of flame, was fed and continued to burn for the next two days while outside the storm raged on.

The first morning it ended he took her aside and said, 'Come on, let's you and me sneak away and make our own expedition to this famous waterfall. Then when the others get organized and ask us again, we can just say, "Oh, that? We've seen it." '

Brent reached forward and untied the scarf from her hair when they were half-way across the inlet, pounding and bouncing on the scintillating waves. 'Let it blow, Karen-mine. I like the way it shines in the sun, all spangled and bright like wet cobwebs.'

Karen howled with laughter, clear and joyous over the sound of the outboard. 'Wet cobwebs? Those, you find in damp bat-caves! You could at least have said "dew-damp gossamer!" '

'Well, maybe that's what I meant, but it looks nice that way.'

The smile she gave him was more radiant than the sparkling, milky-green water out of which, rising steeply, were golden-green mossy bluffs which soared upward until they rolled slightly to a less upright surface to support the lush, dense growth of evergreens. The trees grew so verdantly that from the vantage point of a half-mile out, they seemed to be a rough-textured drapery of green hung in folds from the deep purple cornice of the distant mountains under the pale blue ceiling of the sky. One of the folds in the curtain of green was caught up and hung suspended for all time, a hanging valley, and from this tumbled a jabot of white lace which came down and down and down until it met with an unseen obstacle and literally squirted out for a hundred feet until it fell straight toward the trees below.

Could it be possible that she heard its muted thunder all this distance away? Could she really see the motion of the frothing water as it pulsed and ebbed in surging force, building, building, building behind some unseen dam and then spurting forth to fling itself onto the shelf midway in its path and squirt like a gigantic god-child's toy, drenching the forest in a spume of spray?

She watched in awe, feeling the majesty of this place, the grandeur of the enfolding mountains, the height and breadth of the sky and felt herself growing, not smaller, more insignificant as she may have expected, but larger, more complete, part of the spectacular surroundings, as strong as the mountains, as tall and straight as the trees, as powerful as the force of water which tumbled and flew into tatters to rejoin the main body again and become part of the whole. She felt a greatness within herself, and paradoxically, a humility.

'Well?' said a warm voice in her ear as a chin came to rest on her shoulder and warm arms come around her from behind. 'First impressions? Can you put them in words?'

'Not really . . .' His slightly bristly cheek against her own felt so good! She tried to talk of what she was feeling, but it was too big a thing to verbalize.

'Then you do feel it, too,' he said, rocking her as the waves were rocking their small boat. 'I hoped you would . . . the sense of being part of it all, and the sense of being humbled. A paradox, as you say, but if you think deeply, it begins to make sense. We aren't just among the great, we are part of the great. Alone, we are each just one individual. It is when we find ourselves joining with other individuals, the trees, the mountains, the water and the sky, I count them, too, then we become a segment of the whole and therein lies the greatness.'

Karen nodded slowly in agreement. 'We

find harmony. That was the word I wanted before.'

'I'm glad we came alone,' he said. 'It wouldn't have been like this in a crowd of oohing and ahing people. Is that why you wouldn't join them?'

'How could it have been?' Karen asked. 'I didn't know then what we were going to see, to experience. No, it was because I refused to accept for both of us, only accepted for myself and saw the invitation snatched back unless I could be an appendage of a man . . . you. I don't want to be only welcome that way.'

'No,' he said, sitting back, removing the warmth of his body from her. 'I suppose you wouldn't. We'd better go back now.'

He dropped her at the hotel wharf and left with a smile and a wave to go off on one of his solitary pursuits, the sound of the outboard dying slowly as it disappeared around a point along the shore. She retired to bed without his having returned and awoke in the morning having dreamt of him for what must have been the entire night, to find him waiting for her at the breakfast table, pleasant, companionable and friendly.

When is he going to mention that famous 'last alternative' of his, she wondered as the day progressed with no word from him on the subject. It was not until evening came that he did.

The night was soft and warm, stars shone, a sickle of the waning moon laid a tracery of silver across the dark water, danced up the beach to drop sequins through the branches of a tree into Karen's hair. Brent lifted a strand, chuckled and said, 'Wet cobwebs.' Then, dropping it, he moved back a bit, cleared his throat as if suddenly nervous.

'Karen . . . do you think you could live in isolation, far from civilization, far from home, and be happy?'

'I know I could, Brent. I've come to love *this* place.'

'This place has plenty of gaiety in it. The place I'm talking about doesn't, except for the fun and gaiety we make for ourselves. We try, Karen-mine, but there is something missing. I think what's missing is you. There's such a need for someone with love to give, compassion, empathy, all things you have. I need you . . . Oh, Karen! How I need you!

'I told you about Greta, who wants to dance, and can't. There's Louise, who has a terrible need to look upon beauty because she thinks she has none of it herself. It's there, shining out for everyone else to see, but she can't see it. And then there's Mary . . . she's blind, along with everything else, and longs for a soft voice to read stories to her.

'The first time I saw you . . . the night before we met . . . I saw your face, and recognized you for what you are inside. And then I saw you walk, and knew you'd be a dancer. When I heard your voice I told myself that you would be going with me if I had to fight off a husband, a family, an entire world to have you! That's why I was so angry, so rough on you. I was so afraid that you were going to disappoint me, Karen, and then in a very short while I knew you would never do that.

'I know now that you don't want to be an appendage, Karen, but would you . . . could you accept a partnership? I need you, they need you! I've only mentioned three . . . three of the girls. There are the boys, too, they have needs I can't even begin to comprehend, but you, with your mate tenderness, w . . . Karen! Karen? What is it? Why are you laughing? Karen! Stop!'

But she could not stop. The laughter came in great, whooping gales, tearing from her lungs as she shook in paroxysms of something which was not mirth! 'Girls? Boys? Children? You want me to care for children? Me? That's awful! Oh, Brent! You don't know what you're saying! I can't! I can't!'

He shook her until her teeth rattled. 'Quit it! For Christ's sake, Karen! Stop it! Yes, I want you to look after children! What's so funny about that? You say you can't? I don't know what you mean! Why can't you?'

'I just can't! Oh, Brent, you have to understand! I simply can not! Oh, come back! Come back! Brent! You have to listen to me!'

But he was not listening, he was not trying to understand. He was striding away, hands shoved deep in pockets, head scrunched down between his shoulders and she watched until he disappeared into the dark night.

A long time later Karen was walking through the hall toward her room. She was numb, hardly able to see, to think, and when she bumped into Lois and made no sound, only stepped aside while staring blankly at the other woman, Lois gasped out her name, took Karen's arm and gently steered her into her own private sitting room.

She knelt before Karen, rubbing the cold hands and arms then wrapped her in a blanket, forced brandy between her teeth, spoonful by spoonful, wishing she dared leave her and go in search of Brent. It was a long time before Karen showed any signs of recovery, and by then it was too late to go in search of anyone.

'It really scares me, you know' were the words Karen spoke conversationally as if in the middle of a dialogue. Lois did not understand but knew that something was about to occur, something which would either bring Karen out of this prison of her own making, or would sink her so deep into its deepest dungeon that she might never emerge. She prayed that Brent would come, but even as she did so, knew that he had somehow triggered this and would not. She was alone, and the sense of responsibility was horrifying! Still, she must carry it through.

Lois drew in a deep breath and said, 'It scares you?' in a tone as casual as the one Karen had used. The girl stared at her and through her and made no reply. As expressionlessly as she could, Lois asked, 'What scares you, dear?'

'The vacuum.' The reply came on a faint note of surprise, as though Lois should have known. Karen's eyes focused on Lois, burning with a passion of pain which was hurtful to behold. 'The awful, expansive vacuum of a desert. It is unending. There will never be anything else! I thought there might have been an end to it but the end wasn't real. There's only the lonely desert!'

'Don't deserts offer oases, Karen?'

'Mirages.'

'Not all, dear. Some are substantial.'

'Tina . . .' came out on a long, sobbing breath.

'Tina?' Lois kept her voice very gentle.

'Tina was a mirage.'

'Was she?'

'Was she real?' Karen's question was plaintive, as a child's. The look in her eyes was frightening. 'Was she real?' she asked again, sounding bewildered.

Lois hesitated before asking. 'Was she, Karen? You tell me.'

Karen drew in a long, shuddering breath, held it for a frighteningly long time and when she began to let it out, did so in one agonized moan of a word: 'Yes . . .' And then, as if a dam had broken, she cried, leaning forward, pounding fists on her knees, 'Oh yes! She was real! God! how real she was! Warm and soft and helpless and right from the beginning when she was first mine and they told me she couldn't stay I swore I could keep her, hold her by my love and I tried, God, how I tried and worked over her and prayed over her and cared for her and they were right and I was wrong and there was nothing I could do! She went away like he did and then there was emptiness and they were both mirages in a vacuum and I was going to go to them but he pulled me back and I still want to go because if I don't I'm going to do something . . . *Terrible!*' She screamed the last word and fell forward with her face against Lois's bosom while the woman rocked her and soothed her until at last she was weeping quietly, able to go on more lucidly.

'Martina . . . my daughter was . . . was born seven months after Marty died. She had a congenital heart defect . . . inoperable, they told me, unless she could live long enough to grow stronger, bigger, able to withstand surgery. They said it would take a miracle to keep her alive that long. I guess the world had used up its quota of miracles that year because she died just before Christmas . . . seven months ago. She was just past her second birthday. The operation was scheduled for the first week in January.'

'Ah . . . Karen! What can I say? You know there's nothing, dear . . .'

'I know Lois. And I'm sorry to have loaded you with it. Brent told me . . . about you . . . and why you're here . . . He'd hate me even more if he knew I was with you now, telling you all this.'

'Brent doesn't hate you Karen . . .'

'He does now . . . He asked me to go with him to wherever it is he calls home, to help him, to care for his children . . . and I can't! Lois, I just can't! He didn't know whom he was asking to go with him and if he did know he'd probably want to kill me . . .'

The quiet desperation in her voice was shocking to Lois even after all the other revelations.

'Is it because you . . . wanted to go to your husband and daughter, Karen? Brent would understand that, dear. He's very understanding. A psychologist must be!'

'Is that what he is? But no, he wouldn't be able to understand this! He knows about the other and called me a coward, told me I was too full of self-pity. He hated me for that, was full of contempt, and I could never tell him about this. Lois, Lois! I couldn't be trusted with his children! I have to practically tie myself up, to put myself in a prison because I want to steal someone else's baby!'

The horror and self-loathing she was feeling transmitted itself into her voice, her posture, and she writhed away from Lois's sympathetic grasp.

'No! No, Karen! You do not! Not now! Maybe before, but not now!' How she knew that so positively, Lois could not have said, but she was sure, so sure she could have staked her life on it, and her conviction must have got through the walls of Karen's self-imposed prison for she turned around, looked intently into Lois's eyes for a long moment, a dawning light of belief growing in her own.

'No . . .' she said slowly, wonderingly, 'I don't. I won't do it. I couldn't put another woman through what I went through.' Karen thought deeply for a long time, then, 'I'm still empty inside, but I feel clean, somehow. As if a pus-filled boil had been broken, drained. I'll heal now,' she finished simply.

Later, over their third cup of tea, Lois smiled and said, 'You'll be going with Brent?'

Karen shook her head, her pale hair floating in a cloud, her large brown eyes soft with an easier sadness. 'No, Lois . . . I don't think so.'

'It would be good, Karen.'

'It could be very good. But we'll wait and see what morning brings.'

FOUR

The interminable trip from Cassiare House to Vancouver had been terrible for Karen. She spent most of her time huddled on her bunk in the room she shared with one other woman who, fortunately, wanted only to be on deck in the sunny weather with her boyfriend. In Karen's bag was the note Lois had handed her just before she left . . . a note from Brent, which she accepted with a wildly beating heart full of hope and went away to read on her own.

'Don't blame yourself', the note read. 'It was my fault for allowing my need to see more in you than there really was. They say first impressions are not to be trusted. This, I should have remembered when I found you to be a coward, but because I wanted to believe differently, I did, and in doing so, hurt both of us. All I can say now is be very careful in your search for a new job and if you ever see an advertisement for help in the Graham Foundation Nature Lodge, don't apply.'

The cruellest part was that there had been no greeting, and no signature, just those bald words which were now burned indelibly into the fabric of her being.

She stood by the rail as the boat sailed under Lion's Gate Bridge and let her eyes roam up the hills and gullies of the North Shore, studded with houses and streaked with streets, and remembered the wildness of the place she had so recently left. On her right, as she stood near the bow, was Stanley Park, a mini-wilderness in part, and she knew she would be required to spend many hours in the future wandering those trails to seek balm for her bruised spirits.

That she could do so now was some solace. No longer did she have to fear herself and her own terrible desire to take a child, any child and run away to hide with it. Now she would be able to go to parks, to visit her parents, her sister, brother, and their children. If nothing else, she had that to cling to, that, and the knowledge that she was no longer limited in her choice of a job. Brent had inadvertantly returned the world to her with one hand while snatching away that which made the world good, with the other.

Dr Porter was awaiting her when she disembarked, ready to drive her home and hear all about the vacation.

'Oh, it was lovely!' said Karen with more enthusiasm than she really felt. 'We only had a few wet days and you were right; dancing and swimming, tennis, boating and hiking were just what I needed. See how tanned I am?'

'Hmm, yes, I see.' The doctor navigated the car around a stopped bus and darted into a gap in a faster lane. The car bounced over railroad tracks, turned and bounded into a narrow side street. 'Your colour is better,' she said a few moments later when they were stopped by a red light and she had more chance to examine her passenger. 'You've gained some weight, too.' The light changed, the car jerked forward, and Dr Porter went on: 'There's still room for improvement, though. You're coming home with me for dinner. I also want to tell you about a case you might like to think about. The present nurse leaves in a month, so you've plenty of time to consider. If you run short . . .'

Her sentence was left unfinished as the car drew to a halt and the passenger door was ripped open. 'Mom!' cried Karen, flinging herself into the reaching arms. 'And Dad! Hey, what a great homecoming! But there was no need; I planned to catch the first ferry across tomorrow morning!'

'Karen, Karen, darling, that's wonderful! You can drive back with us . . . If you really want to go?' There was doubt and concern in her mother's face as Karen stood back to look at her. Her father encircled the two of them with his arms, drawing them toward the door.

'I'm glad you feel like going home, honey, but we'll understand if it proves too hard. Let's sleep on it, O.K.?' Karen's conscience smote her. She knew her father had had to say that, to save her mother possible disappointment and hurt if she, Karen, should treat them again as she had at Christmas. Oh, God! What had been wrong with her, to do that terrible thing to her beloved family?

They were in the warm kitchen, then, where delicious smells emanated from the oven and Karen sniffed appreciatively. 'Mmm! Roast beef?' She peeked into the oven then lifted the lid of a pot on top of the stove. 'Broccoli! Boy, this is a royal welcome. All my favourite food and all my favourite people. Speaking of which, where's the prof?'

Frank Lytell hugged his wife as she stumbled against him, her eyes full of joy and disbelief at this wonderful change in their youngest child. At that moment a fifth figure appeared, took the pot-lid from Karen who was still sniffing the broccoli, slapped her hand and said, 'Right here, urchin and you're taking my vegetables off the boil. Get out of my kitchen, the whole lot of you and don't come back 'til you're called! Who's cooking this dinner, anyway?' His bushy grey eyebrows bounced around his wrinkled forehead and his blue eyes danced merrily. He made a mock swing at his wife with a spatula and she danced out of his way, heading for the living room, followed by their guests.

Karen sat on the floor between her parents who were side by side on the sofa. She leaned her arm on her father's knee and her face against her mother's. 'It's so good to be with you again and it'll be even better to be home and with all the others tomorrow.' She sipped her sherry, knocked the ash off her cigarette and sighed happily. Her mother stroked her bright head and smiled down at her.

'It'll be good to have you home, dear. I'll

alert Johnny and Ethel. You won't have to go through what you did at Christmas. They'll get a sitter for Chrissie when they come to see you.'

Karen became utterly still, completely rigid as she turned her face up to stare, shocked, at her mother. 'Oh, Mom,' she whispered at length, her eyes wide in her pale face. 'You knew? Does Johnny know?'

'Karen . . . of course I knew. I'm your mother! I could see how it hurt you to see Ethel with Chrissie. And no, neither she nor Johnny mentioned it to me, so if they knew, they kept it to themselves.'

'Oh, God! You don't know how horribly guilty I felt! I was sure you'd all hate me for . . .'

'Karen!' That was her father, stern. 'We all love you. We know it must have hurt badly to see your sister and brother with their children when you didn't have yours any longer. We understand.'

Knowing she would never be able to relax at home unless she saw this all the way through, Karen said slowly, painfully. 'But I don't think you really do under-stand. I wasn't just jealous of them for having their kids all around them. Ellen's kids don't bother me . . . it was just Chrissie! I actually hated Johnny and Ethel and even worse . . . Oh, Mom, Dad! Forgive me! I wanted to take her! I was sure Ethel neglected her, didn't love her as much as I would have. I wanted to steal my brother's baby!'

Her parents were both holding her, trying to comfort her, but it was Carol Porter who really got through. She dragged the girl upright in the centre of the room and held her by the shoulders. 'For God's sake, girl! Why didn't you tell us this months ago? Oh, you stupid little fool! What kind of training do they give you kids nowadays? Of all the ridiculous things to have eating at you for all these months when if you'd told me I'd have put a stop to your guilt right away!

'Karen, that is a common reaction among women who have lost children. It's a biological thing! Your child was gone from your arms and your whole mind and body cried out to have it replaced. You needed a child the way an addict needs a drug. If Martin had been alive, you'd have been pregnant in six weeks but he wasn't and your mind adopted the next best solution; take one from someone who didn't really need it as much as you did. The fact that Chrissie resembles Martina a lot just made it worse. In your mind she became

Tina, and in that case, what right did Johnny have to her? Of course they neglected her, didn't love her. If they had been the right kind of parents there'd have been no need for you to take Chrissie away from them.'

She ran out of steam and pushed Karen into a chair, perching her plump form on the arm of it. 'But . . . it's *normal?*' Karen could hardly accept this. 'When I ran away at Christmas I thought it would solve things. Stay away from Chrissie until I got over it. But I didn't! It got worse and worse until I was looking at babies in carriages outside stores, left in cars, playing in their own yards. If I'd gone into an active hospital, even onto a different floor, I knew enough of the routine that I could have taken one from pediatrics or the nursery! I couldn't take that risk!'

'The fact that you recognized there was a risk and fought against it, tells me that you were incapable of doing it, Karen,' said her father thoughtfully, and she shot him a grateful glance. Why hadn't she told them all when it first started? Far from the censure she felt she deserved from them for what she had almost done to the entire family, they were giving her help, trying to work this out with her!

'That's right,' said her mother. 'And if you still had those inclinations, you wouldn't have told us about them . . . Carol?'

'Yes, Di. You're both right. Do you still think you're in any danger of it, Karen?'

'No. From the time I first put it into words . . . to your friend . . . and now mine, Lois Granger, the urge was gone. She was so utterly positive that I wouldn't, couldn't do it, that somehow she made me believe it.'

The nine days at her parents' home were a wonderful time of healing, of growing close to her family again. Karen was treated like the prodigal returned. Her sister, Ellen, who lived conveniently next door, kept feeding her! Every time Karen sat down from a boisterous game of some sort with her two nephews and niece, there was Ellen, with cake or pie or ice cream or cookies; large jugs of lemonade, or iced tea, sweet and minty, usually accompanied the plates of goodies.

'Ellen! Knock it off, for pete's sake! I'm going to get fat! I'm surprised you haven't been spending all your spare time making vats and vats of chicken soup!'

Ellen gave her younger sister a crooked

smile. 'There were times, sister-mine . . . there were times . . .'

A horn honked loudly in the driveway. 'Hey, in there! Anybody want to go to the beach?'

It was Johnny, Ethel and Chrissie. In spite of Karen's assurances that the child of the same age and colouring as her own had been would not upset her, Johnny had failed to bring his daughter along on the two visits he and his wife had made to the family home in the past few days. But today they were all here . . .

'Uncle Johnny! Uncle Johnny! You got room for all of us?' That was Larry Junior, Ellen's eldest, yelling as he dashed out of the sprinkler wet and shining in the sun, followed by his brother Peter and his sister, Gay, who, at four years of age was almost as big as six-year-old Peter.

Ellen and Larry's children, spaced almost exactly two years apart, clambered noisily into the open tail-gate of the station wagon and Karen got into the back seat with Ellen. They sat one on either side of the child in the car-seat, the golden beauty of Chrissie echoing the golden beauty that had been Martina and for a moment Karen was near to tears.

The car lurched out into the street and

Ethel turned, grinning at her two sisters-in-law. 'You guys O.K. back there in cookie-crumb land? That rotten little kid between you can't eat a cookie neatly to save her soul!'

That 'rotten little kid' chose that moment to smear her sticky hands in Karen's hair. 'Oh, baby, don't do that,' crooned Karen, gently untangling the fat little fingers from her long tresses, careful not to cut the child. 'Come out of there and let me hold you.' She was about to lift the toddler out of the car-seat when she was stopped by a firm and decisive word from her sister-in-law.

'No!' Then, more gently, 'No, Karen. The seat's belted to the car and she's belted to the seat. Much safer that way than if she were in your lap. You can play with her all you want once we're safe on the beach. The way some people drive around here is enough to make my hair stand on end!'

'Sorry.' Karen was chastened. 'I wasn't thinking.' But now she was. As often as her brother and his wife referred to their only child as that 'rotten little kid', which was very often, they obviously cared a great deal for her safety.

The bedlam in the extreme back of the

wagon was released soon onto the wide expanse of beach and the children ran shrieking into the surf, splashing each other wildly until little Gay came running back, howling that Peter had got her new bathing suit all wet.

'Isn't that what bathing suits are supposed to get?' asked Karen, to whom the tale of woe had been told.

'Yes! But I wanted to do it my ownself!' Gay stomped off, still highly incensed at her brother's nefarious action.

Ethel handed Chrissie to Karen. 'Here, you go swim with your Auntie. I'm going to get a tan if it kills me!'

Karen carried the little girl over the beach toward the water. Johnny caught her just as she entered the surf. 'Put that kid down,' he said. 'She can walk. She's not a baby anymore, Karen!'

'In this?' Karen gestured toward the foot-high slop rolling up the beach and sucking out again. 'You expect her to walk in that? She'd be knocked over!'

'Won't kill her. She can swim, too.'

'Swim? At two and a half? Johnny!'

He took his daughter from Karen and went out until the water was up to his armpits. 'You back off about ten feet,' he instructed Karen. She complied, heart in her mouth, as he let the little child go and she, gurgling, spluttering and quite happy about it all, dog-paddled to her aunt who caught her and held her closely, feeling tears sting at the backs of her eyes. If she had a baby like this she'd never put her in such danger! Oh, how could he? This warm, tiny body with her clinging arms, so round, so soft, so precious! being exposed to all that water, far over her depth . . .

But that warm, precious little body was struggling and squawling, 'Swim, Auntie! Swim! Chrissie swim!' and Johnny, eyes threatening, was saying, 'Send her back! She wants to swim back to me, Kat!'

It was the use of that childhood name more than anything which broke Karen out of the spell she was under. She let the child slide down into the water and removed her hands. With misted eyes she watched her dog-paddle back to her father. Suddenly Karen's vision cleared as Johnny caught the child in a bear-hug, and she called across the ten feet of emptiness between herself and her brother and his child, 'Look out Olympics! Here comes Chrissie Lytell!'

Johnny grinned at her and when the child had had enough, they waded ashore together. Johnny put an arm around his sister's shoulders, squeezed her tightly and said, 'O.K. now?'

'O.K. now, Johnny.'

'That's my Kat!'

And so went her first vacation at home in well over two years. During Tina's short life-span, Karen had never taken the baby home; the state of her health was too precarious for the risking of even such a short trip, but now, with the horror of her terrible urge behind her, Karen could relax and enjoy the special closeness of family life.

When the time came to leave she did so with a light heart, knowing that she would be able to return whenever she had time from the demands of her job, and knowing now just what that job was to be:

Karen was going to Brent.

As yet she knew nothing about the place, only that he was there, and where he was was where she had to go. It never occured to her that she might be wrong . . .

She smiled to herself as the ferry docked at Horseshoe Bay and she started her car, preparing to drive off and into the city. 'Be very careful', he had written, and being a psychologist, he must have known what he was doing; he had known that she would come to him when she had had time to think it out. Why else would he have been so careful to give her the name of the place?

Her heart sang gaily; so did Karen as her tires spun along the Upper Levels Highway, soaring along the brinks of cliffs, hanging on spider-web bridges over chasms, dipping down into valleys and climbing again almost to the sky where there was a view, especially laid on for those light of heart, of the sparkling city, washed by a recent rain of its smog and smoke, as clean and fresh as this new-born day in her new-born life.

Suddenly her singing heart lurched as did her zooming car. She righted the last but could do nothing about the first, and the song on her lips died in mid-bar as she faced one inescapable fact: She did not know where the Graham Foundation Nature Lodge was!

'. . . I haven't a clue, Mrs Jamison. Why don't you check the Public Library, or even the Yellow Pages? If it's a locally administered foundation there must be offices here, but it could be from the east, or from Victoria.'

Darn! Karen had been so sure that the Nurses' Registry would be able to tell her;

wasn't it likely that they had provided staff for it? Seemed not!

A listing of Corporations and Foundations provided by the Library was only slightly more helpful. For the Graham Foundation there was a number to call, but at the other end of the line was a trust company switchboard. After a few confused exchanges between herself and an operator, it was established that yes, the trust company did, indeed, administer the Graham Foundation, but there seemed to be no one authorized to give out information. After much chatter back and forth, it was at last agreed that Karen could call at the trust company's offices and speak to Mr Hobbs, who might be able to help her.

'You simply wish to visit this place, Mrs Jamison?' Clearly Mr Hobbs thought her sanity was in doubt. 'Mr Cookson, the director, invited you, but neglected to tell you how to reach it?' Now, it seemed, it was her veracity that was in doubt! Well . . . she was forced to face the fact Mr Hobbs wasn't far wrong! 'Might I suggest,' he went on kindly in his dry, dusty voice, 'that you write to him and have the invitation confirmed? I can see no harm in giving you the mailing address.'

A road map showed that the place where Brent's mail was picked up from was a fair drive from the city. From there, she would just have to play it by ear. If nothing else presented itself, she would probably end up crawling into his mailbox and waiting, she thought whimsically, wondering if it wouldn't just be easier to write to Lois and ask her. But no. She couldn't do that. Her pride, of which she still had a small amount, wouldn't allow it, for if he simply tossed her out on her ear, she didn't want anyone else to know about it!

The next morning she was back on the Upper Levels Highway, speeding toward Horseshoe Bay, not, this time for the trip to Nanaimo, but to sail across Howe sound to the Sechelt Penninsula. The ferry, the Sechelt Queen, was loading as she drove up, and the forty-five minute trip was time on her hands, time in which she could be doing nothing herself toward getting to Brent. It was torture! but at last the ferry docked and she drove off to be met by a sign saying that the next ferry, at Earl's Cove, just beyond the place where she was to turn, was fifty miles away, an 'easy two-hour drive.' Two hours? To do fifty miles? Who were they trying to kid?

Karen sped past a line of slow moving cars, swung into a curve and hit the brakes, knowing that no one had been trying to kid anyone! This road was murder!

Switch-back followed switch-back. Slow trucks ground their way up hills; there was no place to pass for miles. The road wound into towns, and out again, and oh! at last, a place to pass this truck! But, darn it, there was oncoming traffic! By the time the way ahead was clear, there were more curves and corners, and more and more and more! Thank goodness for small mercies! That truck turned off the highway at Sechelt and Karen was free to drive along a road which was broader now, fewer curves and grades, fewer houses and towns and in one spot, when she did not need it, a long passing lane as the road climbed an easy hill.

Further on it narrowed once more and as she swooped down a long, curving hill there was a checker-board sign indicating a right-angle turn with a sign saying slow to fifteen, which she did not do, a mistake she was not to repeat for the rest of the drive. When a sign told her to slow to ten miles per hour, she did exactly that, fully convinced now that the Department of

Highways knew far better than she just what was possible on this tortuous strip of road.

Halfmoon Bay, Secret Cove, Seven Isles, and yes, there were islands out there in that water visible through a break in the trees . . . take the sign's word for it . . . not safe to try to count! . . . Silver Sands, Madeira Park and a pink hotel called Rigger's Roost. Coffee time and a place with a name like that just had to be investigated!

On the road again . . . Oyster Bay, Kleindale, an unexpected high-school stuck bleak and dry and lonely in the middle of an unexpected pocket-prairie which gives way to more and more and more winding road and in time a view of two lakes, one higher and smaller than the long, narrow strip of water far below her . . . did the smaller, higher one drain into the larger, lower one? Who knows, and who cares? Brent is somewhere ahead. Keep driving!

The highway sneaked up on the smaller of the lakes, ducked across a narrow gap with water on both sides and swept along, sometimes high, sometimes low, sometimes almost out of sight of it, and then, leaving, rushed into the first straight stretch in ages . . . must have been all of a mile long before a curve brought her to the sign she had been seeking: Egmont, four miles . . .

Turning right onto the narrow strip of black-top which tumbled immediately into a dip and a swing, she braked sharply to avoid a pothole and a truck, narrowly missing a tree which seemed to spring out of nowhere. If the main highway had been a nightmare, surely this was a bad trip . . . in the drug sense of the word! A high, open area with only the most rudimentary of guardrails gave view to an expanse of open water. Lake or ocean Karen did not know and did not stop to find out; a sign said, 'Caution, Logging Trucks', and she used extreme caution, far more than the teenager-filled convertible which crowded her onto the narrow shoulder with laughs of glee from its occupants.

Another body of water; North Lake. How original can you get? Where are East, West and South? Not here obviously, for the next one is 'Waugh', and then in hardly any time at all, the termination of the road at a long wharf, a store, some houses and not much else.

Questions elicited varying responses:

'Don't know. I'm an American tourist. Just pulled in to gas up the boat.' and, 'Nature Lodge? Whaddya want with a place like that? Stick around here, baby, and learn *my* nature!' But at last, 'Oh, yes. The Colonel's place. It was converted a few years back to a home for crippled Indian kids. You want to go there?' This man, like Mr Hobbs, seemed to doubt her sanity, but he did become more helpful when she explained that she was a nurse. Oh, that magic word! Open sesame to almost any place!

Thanks to the kindly help of the man, she soon found herself in a bright blue water-taxi which bubbled its fumey breath into the water of the bay, gurgled past moored fishing boats and pleasure boats, past row-boats skimming and swimmers splashing and so out into the inlet where the boy in charge of it opened the throttles with a grin and sent Karen thudding solidly back into her seat, victim of many 'Gees'.

'Like it?' he hollered over the roar, and she grinned, feeling her hair streaming back, 'Love it!'

And she did. The sun picked up highlights from the water, bouncing them into her eyes but sunglasses dulled the perfection too much to be borne. Golden bluffs of moss rolled up out of the water into steeply wooded hillsides of green which grew and grew and grew to become purple, distant mountains, some with new snow-caps on this crisp September afternoon, some with aged glaciers clinging to their rocky slopes.

For over an hour they streamed along, the boiling white wake rolling out to become black and smooth as it pushed toward the shores, far on Karen's left, near on her right, where the waves from the boat's passage frothed up the walls of the inlet. While her heart sang a song of thanksgiving that she was going to Brent, her mind was taking each impression, filing it, comparing it, and coming to the impossible conclusion that she had been here before.

She called a comment to this effect to the boy and he yelled back, 'Sure! All these inlets look alike! Ask any tourist!'

Ahead, must surely be the end of this one; the mountains folded in together as neatly as fingers on praying hands. There could be no further water to fly along, but as they approached, the mountains parted, giving way to another, and in time, yet another reach, bordered on both sides by the high, steep mountains with ribbons of water flying down their flanks.

The noise died to a gutteral rumble as the boat genuflected dramatically in obesience to the majesty of the hills which slid back here to admit a wide bay with a large house and some out-buildings set back under a canopy of shading maples. To the wharf the bay offered, the boy steered his craft, and in a short, too-short, minute, he was unloading Karen's luggage while she fumbled in her bag for her fare, suddenly afraid to let his friendly face go out of her life. She was as unsure now as she had been sure, earlier, of her welcome. But he was reversing away, waving, calling, 'Just go on up. Someone'll come down for your bags. So long, nurse!'

Karen flicked a glance at the small launch tied bobbing at the wharf in the waves of the departing taxi and began the climb which took her to the wide, shady verandah running across the front of the main building. As she neared a door, a voice said in utter and complete disgust. 'Naw! It ain't Brent! I told you he's not comin' back! It's just some woman!' A child cried, there was the sound of a slap, and a feminine voice saying sharply, angrily, 'Stop that Freddy!' and the door was half-opened to reveal a harried, gaunt woman of indeterminate age with frowsy hair and veined, purple cheeks.

'You took your sweet time getting here,' she whined, 'but then, I suppose I should be grateful she even bothered to send you. I didn't think she would. What's your name?'

'Karen Jamison . . . is . . . is B . . . Mr Cookson here?' Although, from hearing the comment of the first person who had spoken, she was almost sure he was not, she simply had to ask!

'Another one of them, are you? Come here all fired up to work for the handsome Mr Cookson and then find out that's all you get . . . work! You won't last any longer than any of the others. He doesn't see nurses as wimmen. You better come in and see your room if you really want to stay. He's not here just now.' The woman turned and snarled. 'Go on! Get yourselves out of here. No one wants to see your ugly faces!'

When the sound of a closing door had been heard, the woman admitted Karen to a small entry-hall with tables, a jug of wild flowers and a few chairs. There were three doors leading off it in addition to the one she had just come through.

'Uh . . . what's your name?' she asked pleasantly, and had to suppress a hysterical desire to laugh at the reply.

'Mrs Muffin.' Anything less like a muffin Karen had never seen. The housekeeper, if that were what she was, led the way down a long, empty corridor and opened a door, showing Karen a nice room with a bright spread on the bed, cupboards, dresser, desk, two easy chairs and wide windows open to the breeze which blew in scented by the forest. 'You better stay here. I'll bring your stuff and some lunch for you, too.'

'But the children . . . the staff . . . ?' Why was this place, presumably filled with children, so quiet?

'The kids you'll see plenty of. You can wait. Staff?' Mrs Muffin gave a bitter little laugh. 'Ain't none. Didn't she tell you? Two of the aides left before she did, and when she went there was only me 'n'one aide'n Louise, but she don't count, she's sort of one of the kids.' Leaving Karen even more confused than before, she stumped off, returning in a few minutes with a bowl of luke-warm soup, an indifferent sandwich and a cup of revolting coffee on a tray with a dirty cloth. She dumped it on the desk without a word and went out. Karen was choking the sandwich down when the woman came in with the baggage.

'I could have done that myself, Mrs Muffin,' she said, but the angry reply she got made her sink back, wondering what she had got into.

'Just like all the others. Start out nice as pie, end up mean and pushy. Forget it, nurse, I know yer kind!'

'Mrs Muffin . . . I think you should know I haven't been hired to . . .'

'To take that kind of talk from a house-keeper?' finished the old woman sarcasti-cally. 'Well I wasn't hired to do a nurse's job, neither, and if you're here to do a job, you'd better get on with it. The office is the next door on your right. You'll find all the case hist'ries in the files. You'll need to know what yer gettin' into.'

Some time later when she was called by the still bad-tempered housekeeper to dinner, Karen did have a little more idea of what she was getting into! The histories had revealed a grim story of twenty-two lives filled with horror, deprivation and loss. These children of Brent's had been through more than she thought human beings should be called upon to withstand. Tales of neglect, of starvation, of beatings, of burnings, or debilitating vitamin deficiencies and in each one, a disabling deformity, enough in itself to have put a child through hell. There had been, in many cases . . . no, most cases, a lack of proper medical attention but most of all seemed to be the lack of love . . . love that all Brent's neat notes ordered be given in abundance, even when it was rejected and tossed back in the faces of the staff.

Fully prepared to enter a room containing crippled children looking to her for love and compassion, Karen hesitated at the door, listening to the mad screaming, the angry verbal attacks and counter-attacks, the wailing and shouting, all of which died abruptly into a sullen silence as she entered the dining room. She stood stock still while all those pairs of suspicious, acrimonious black eyes stared at her with unconcealed animosity and felt her courage draining out of her, felt her smile of greeting waver under the wall of antipathy which dealt her a sledge-hammer blow to the solar plexus.

Where were all those poor, deformed little children whose minds, whose bodies, whose hearts were crying out for the all-encompassing, all-healing love of Karen Jamison? Where were they? Who were these bitter, hardened hostiles who now faced her? And where, oh where was Brent?

FIVE

That there were children here, there was no denying; that they were crippled, even deformed, was also undeniable. One had only to see the wheel-chairs, the crutches, the bent and twisted limbs, to know that. But that they were helpless, in need of loving care and kindness, was a rank figment of some warped imagination!

Karen put her smile back on and slipped into a vacant place between two small girls and said to the table at large. 'Hello, everyone. My name is Karen. Suppose we start on my left and each of you tell me your name?'

There wasn't a word, a smile, just that stulifying silence and those expressionless faces under straight, black hair. The black, unreadable eyes with the oriental cast stared back at her from their secretive houses inside visages with high cheekbones, flattened noses and sullen, down-turned mouths.

Mrs Muffin entered with a trolley of plates. Each plate was plunked rudely in front of a child. Each portion was exactly the same size, in exactly the same position. A heap of what looked like boiled ground beef sat in an anemic, thin gravy, a scoop of diced beets ran redly into a pile of lumpy mashed potatoes and a mass of wilted lettuce with a few pieces of tomato sitting sadly on top comprised the main meal. Plates of bread and glasses of milk, with coffee for Karen, were added on the housekeeper's next trip.

Karen tried again to talk to the children, and after giving them a brief, edited version of her own personal history, to which no one seemed to pay the slightest attention, she was finally forced either to give up or start asking direct questions. She chose the latter course.

'I'm told there are twenty-two people here and all I can count are twenty. Have some children left recently?'

One boy, whose eyes were more bold than sullen, replied, 'Nope.'

Not greatly encouraged, Karen pressed on. 'Where are the missing people?'

A shrug was her answer.

'Who is missing?' she persevered.

'Lou. And Tommy and Jill.' Was he talking with his mouth full simply because he knew what her reaction was likely to be, or because he had never been taught differently?

'Don't they want to eat?'

'They are. Lou just don't want to eat with you.'

This conversation stopper had the desired effect and no more was said until after they had consumed the lumpy custard provided by the bad-tempered housekeeper, and then the first comment was not really a spoken word.

The bold-eyed boy leaned back in his chair, rubbed his stomach and cracked a loud, disgusting belch, looking directly at Karen as he did so. Elbows poked ribs all down the table, subdued titters could be heard in the silence. 'My,' said Karen admiringly, 'are you an Eskimo? I thought there were only Indians here!'

'I am a full blooded Haida,' said the boy pridefully. 'We can burp, too!'

'So I heard.' She frowned consideringly as she stood up, pushing her chair back and automatically handing a pair of crutches to the child on her right. 'That's quite odd, though. I'd always heard the Haida were a strong and proud race . . .'

He was drawn, as she had hoped he would be! 'Who says we aren't?' His sticks clacked against his chair as he got to his feet as quickly as he could.

'Why, no one, really,' said Karen. 'It was just your own actions which made me doubt it. Eskimos, you see, only belch to show appreciation for a good meal, and I was surprised that a Haida would be less prideful.' On that note, she left the room, leaving the children behind her to figure out what she meant.

They came, one by one, small group by small group, to sit in varying poses and moods in the living room where Karen had curled up in a chair by the fire she had lit. She had a magazine open in her lap and now and then she turned a page, giving every appearance of enjoying an article or story. It took a long time, but at last a small chair was sidled up near her.

'That was a bad dinner, wasn't it nurse?'

Karen put her book down, smiled at the small, female face in front of her. She nodded. 'What's your name?'

'Julie. I'm eight.'

'Are you hungry, Julie?' The child nodded. Karen wasn't at all surprised. Few of the children had managed to eat the entire meal, and of those who had, the teenagers, mostly, they had done so as though stoking furnaces, not bodies, and had shown no enjoyment . . . again, not surprising. 'I'll go and see if Mrs Muffin will let me make some cocoa and get some cookies. We all need a bedtime snack.' As though she and Julie were conspirators, Karen grinned secretly at the little girl.

There was no return of the smile, but a slight lessening of the tension in the small, chair-bound body. 'Will you please tell the others . . . the ones who aren't here, that we're having a party in the living room?' Again, she was given a solemn nod.

The kitchen, when Karen arrived, was empty. The dishes had obviously been done, the table and the counter scrubbed clean, and on the table, propped against a large sugar bowl, stood a stiff piece of paper. Karen felt sick, knowing what it contained almost before reading it.

'Nurse,
    I'm an old woman and I'm tired. I've seen too many nurses come and go and this time I'm not waiting for you to sneak off, leaving me holding the bag the way she did. The one aide we had left should have come back today and she didn't so she probably won't. He'll

114

be back in a day or so and you can tell him he'll find the boat at Johnstone's.'

The note was unsigned and Karen stood gripping the back of a chair while her head reeled and spun and panic overtook her in great, gulping waves . . . Visions of all those pairs of accusing eyes facing her over an empty breakfast table were superseded by visions of a phalanx of chairs crowding her into a corner, pinning her there while she was beaten and bruised by fourteen pairs of crutches and a strange girl, Louise by name, said, 'I won't eat with her! I won't eat with her!'

She ran her hands into her hair, shuddering, and choked again and suddenly she was laughing with a touch of hysteria at the stupidity of her imagination.

First things first, Karen, she told herself, opening cupboards and searching. You promised that mob in there cocoa and cookies, and you'd better produce, girl, or that little fit of imagination might not be too far wrong! When the 'party' was ready, she wheeled the cart into the living room and found the population swelled considerably.

There were a few strained smiles of thanks, a few murmured words, but for the most part her offering was accepted with suspicion and impersonal dislike tempered only by hunger or greed. When every child had been served, Karen curled up once more in her chair, gazing out over the heads of her charges and began speaking quietly holding her voice low so that the children were forced to pay close attention if they wanted to hear.

'Boys and girls, I can see that you're not very happy about having me here. I'm sorry about that, but there's not much I intend to do about it. I will not leave. I will not be chased out by bad manners, or poor behaviour. Most of you don't need me or any other nurse, but I'm going to stay for the sake of those who do. You bigger ones could probably all take care of yourselves, but I don't think you could do much for the younger kids.

'I came to help but I can't if I don't know what each one of you requires. Oh, I read all your case histories in the office . . .' she snapped her fingers . . . 'they tell me that much! They are just words on paper, they are not people with arms and legs and chairs and braces and crutches and special shoes and likes and dislikes. Papers with words are no good to me, just as I'll be no good to any of you unless you tell me what you need me for. While you all talk it over and decide which of you need me, I'll clear this up and wash the cups. See you all in a little while.'

When she returned she paused outside the door, surprised. There was the sound of roaring laughter and one voice crying out. 'But I don't think you should have, Freddy! What if she gets mad, ties them to the beds like *she* did?'

'Aww . . . shaddup, Margo! If she does, Lou'll untie 'em! An' if she gets mad at Lou, *I'll* take care of her . . .' The sneering threat in Freddy's tone chilled Karen . . . Freddy . . . so that was the name of the bold-eyed boy. She recognised the voice. Margo's she did not, but filed the name for future reference, and making quite a lot of noise about it, fumbled with the door knob as she opened it.

There was one desultory game of monopoly being played, and the number of children present had dwindled. 'Hi,' said Karen. 'I'm all finished. Is anyone ready to go to bed yet, and if so, who needs help?'

Freddy answered, his eyes glittering meanly. 'Mike, Peter, Paul and Grant have gone to get washed. Paul and Mike need help getting into bed and Peter needs a diaper.' He hooted with laughter at this last bit of information but Karen managed to keep her face expressionless, betraying none of the shock she felt.

'Fine,' she said levelly. 'I'll go now. Margo?' A girl of about fourteen looked up involuntarily. 'Will you come with me please, to show me around?'

She followed the quickly moving chair into the dormitory annex. Margo stopped by a door marked 'Linen Room', and said in a harsh, unhappy voice, 'This is where you'll find the diapers. Get enough for five . . . that's ten of those torn sheet pieces.'

Karen put a hand on Margo's shoulder. 'Oh, come on! Wasn't Freddy joking?'

'Nope. Miss Lowe said the ones that couldn't get up at night by themselves had to be diapered. We're supposed to have an aide on duty by the crying room but two of them quit and Miss Lowe said the last one, the nice one, Jenny, would have to sleep at night so she could help in the day time. Even after Lou had told her that Brent was bringin' a nice nurse and she got mad and left, Jenny wanted to stay up at night but the dragon . . . Mrs Muffin . . . wouldn't help her much and she couldn't do it. So it was still diapers.

I can get myself in and out of my chair so I'm not one of them who have to be diapered. If I did I'd get so mad, like Frankie does, and I'd end up sleeping in the crying room,' she finished vehemently.

'What is this crying room?'

'That's where we go when we first come here if we're mad and scream and fight a lot. I spent three days there,' she said with some pride. 'Brent said I was a tough nut to crack even though I wasn't very old. I bit him.' She frowned, as if that part of the memory didn't make her too happy, and changed the subject back to that of the diapers.

'The one's who need 'em are Julie and Flo, over there, the names are all on the doors, and Peter, there, Billy and Frankie. Billy's going to put up a fight but you can handle him. Frankie's the one you won't be able to, so you'll have a wet bed to change in the morning if he can't make it. You gave him hot chocolate so he won't.' Was that pleasure in her tone?

Karen strained her memory of the files she had read. Wasn't Frankie one of the teenagers? And Billy . . . or was it Bill, there were two of them, was ten or eleven! Julie and Flo, she seemed to recall, were among the youngest, and Peter, she knew, was eleven!

'Darnit! There's just no *way* I'm going to diaper kids their ages! Margo, there has to be another way! Help me think! Is there a room I could use to sleep in . . . a vacant room, maybe, near enough so I could hear someone call out?'

Margo looked up at the flushed face of the nurse, surprised. The nurse looked mad! Mad at whom? At her? It wasn't her fault these kids couldn't get into their wheelchairs alone, was it? Suddenly she was sick with fear of what would happen when the nurse started making her rounds . . .

'No!' she blurted. 'There's no place at all! Can I go now?' Without waiting for a reply she bolted, hands working frantically to push the wheels of her chair, rolling it rapidly away leaving Karen staring after her, wondering what she had done.

The room of the four boys who reputedly wanted help was the first on her list, but still she hesitated by the linen room, loathe to gather up diapers and take them along with her. Her eyes, roving up and down the corridor, lit on the door of the crying room. She crossed the hall, opened it, and found herself in a tiny, cell-like cubicle with only a narrow, iron bed. There was no window, no cupboard nor chest of drawers, no picture to mar the starkness of the pale green walls, but it had that bed, and it was vacant, two very necessary items in her estimation! This would do!

She read the list of names on the door of the room beside it: Mike, Peter, Paul, Grant. Right, these ones had at least requested help. Therefore they would get help first. She opened the door.

The floor was littered with torn comics, toys, books, stuffing from foam pillows and bedding! It was a disaster area! And Karen knew then what Freddy and Margo had been arguing about. Freddy, bless his hateful little soul, had put them up to it! The four of them sat there in their chairs as innocent as babes. 'Hi, nurse,' said one, 'we was playin' while we waited for you to help us into bed.' One other one lolled loosely sideways in his chair; his poor little damaged spine was incapable of holding him upright . . . Another, with severe burn-scars twisting the tendons of his left arm and leg just fiddled with a pillow case while the fourth sat shaking uncontrollably, his poor little knees bouncing up and down under the blanket which covered them.

Karen waded through the room, kicking things aside as she did so, her hands were on the hips of her jeans and her hair was coming undone. She was almost ready to come undone! but to the boys, she looked less like a nurse than an avenging angel. What was she going to do to them? For the first time they each began to doubt that Freddy had been right; that she would go away if they showed her they didn't want her, but wanted the nurse Brent had said he'd bring! What if she tied them to their beds the way Miss Lowe had? Peter, who had trouble breathing at the best of times, began to rasp painfully.

'Mike!' One boy looked up, eyes wide, and Karen knew which one Mike was. 'So you were playing, were you?' He was the one who had spoken. 'I'm glad. The mess in this room makes me glad. It answers a question of mine . . . what can such poor, crippled little boys do for amusement? Well now I know. And it seems that not one of you is as crippled as you'd like me to believe. Grant, sit up straight!' Ah, lucky guess! The lolling one jerked himself upright. 'Paul, stop shaking your knees like that. I know a genuine spastic tremor when I see it, and brother, that *ain't* one! Peter, if you're capable of tearing up pillows, you'd better be pretty good at restuffing them or you're going to have a very uncomfortable night. You sound asthmatic to me. You can be doing that while Mike remakes the beds and Paul and Grant lean over and pick up every piece of paper and junk from the floor. I wouldn't want to trip when I come in at night if you call me to help you get up. I'll be back in half an hour to lift you into your beds. This room had better be ship-shape.'

She leaned weakly against the door when she had pulled it shut behind her and was gratified to hear a sharp whisper, 'Come on! Hurry up! She meant it!' The whisper was accompanied by sounds of activity and another whisper, a wheezing one, 'She said she'd help me get up at night! Think she meant that?'

The half hour she had given the boys was taken up by seeing other children to bed, tucking in those of the younger ones who seemed to be less likely to bite, and even dropping a kiss here and there, only to see each one wiped off angrily until she said, 'Oh, how nice. If you'd give me a kiss, I'd rub it in, too,' and offered her cheek to small Julie. The child reddened but refused to kiss Karen who smiled gently and wished them all a goodnight, reiterating the information that she would be sleeping in the crying room if anyone should want her.

The room of the boys, when she returned, was not exactly ship-shape, but far, far better than what it had been. Karen spoke pleasantly as she untied braces and laces, lifted limp or rigid bodies from chair to bed and repeated her promise that she would be available all night long. As she had done with the other rooms, she left the door to this one ajar and called a soft 'Goodnight!' Only one voice replied . . . asthmatically . . . 'Night, Karen,' making her feel she had won a major victory.

With lighter steps she checked out the length of the corridor, seeing some lights still on as older kids read for a while or carried on low-voiced conversations; probably, she decided, discussing her, but that was to be expected.

She yawned, tired out, and wished she could crawl into that narrow little bed in the crying room, but knew she had one more thing to do: make sure there was plenty of food in the kitchen for breakfast in the morning . . .

There were eggs in one of the two fridges, bacon in the other, there was cereal, both dry and for cooking, there was frozen orange juice in large cans in the massive deep freeze along with meat and vegetables and fruit, the cupboards were stocked with every conceivable need in the form of packaged mixes, cans and dehydrated packs, including powdered milk, jugs and jugs of which, mixed up, were in one of the fridges, but of bread, there was no sign at all! How could she prepare a proper breakfast for her charges without bread? Of course, she could make hotcakes, she reasoned, but what, then, would she do for lunch? There would have to be something quick and easy, she knew, because somewhere, she was going to be forced to find time to get this large place cleaned up.

Before those thoughts could drag her down, she began the necessary preparations for making the bread. When the dough had been set to rise she dashed to the dormitory wing to listen for any calls from the children, peek in doors here and there and check, but, finding all quiet, ran back to the kitchen and started an enormous batch of cookies, knowing she had to stay up until the bread was done, and reasoning that her time may as well be spent productively.

As each tray of cookies came out of the oven, she would run back to the children, check, then dash to the warm, scented kitchen. When the last cinnamony disc had been placed to cool on a rack, Karen took a large roast from the freezer, seasoned it and put it in the hot oven before punching her bread down and putting it in pans.

The roast was making a delicious aroma when the bread had risen high enough to go into two of the large ovens and, after placing the loaves in to bake, Karen sat down with a large cup of hot, sweet tea and a plate of still-warm cookies. She sipped and nibbled, listening to the crackling of the meat. Warm and tired in the heat of the kitchen she knew she should go and check on her charges again but the effort . . . was just too . . . much . . .

A hand on her shoulder brought her out of her doze with a startled yelp: 'The kids! The bread!'

'You're bakin' bread?' was the equally startled reply from the girl who had awakened Karen. 'I'll check on it. Julie's calling.'

Karen looked blearily at the tall young girl who stood there, staring, as if unbelieving of what she saw, dressed in a plain cotton night-gown. She was barefoot and her hair, skinned back unattractively, was tied with a shoelace, but her large, luminous eyes glowed and shone with a kind of . . . other-worldliness, belying her mouth, a cruel, mangled gash of a hare-lip which had been terribly botched in repair, as had, Karen realized when the girl spoke once more, the cleft palate which so often accompanied hare-lip.

'Please, nurse . . . Julie . . . you didn't diaper her and she needs to go. She's too heavy for me.'

Karen wheeled and dashed for the annexe, helped little Julie and bedded her down with another kiss, this one not being rubbed off . . . or in, and returned to the kitchen to what surely must be Louise, the elusive Louise the kids had mentioned, the Louise of which Brent had told her . . . with beauty shining out for others to see . . .

The aroma was strong in the hallway and Karen realized then how Louise had known where to find her, but it was stronger, more delicious, in the kitchen; the loaves, golden brown and glistening as the girl carefully smeared butter over their tops, wafted their scent throughout the room.

'Thank you, Louise,' said Karen. 'I'm sorry Julie woke you. I've been going back and forth, checking, but I fell asleep and missed hearing her.'

The girl turned from the bread, dropped a buttery piece of paper towel in the garbage can and approached the table hesitantly, an odd, reeling gait drawing Karen's professional eye. Congenital hip deformity, she thought, as incorrectly reduced as had been the lip and palate. Funny there had been no case history for Louise in the files . . .

Louise sat down, eyes on Karen's face, that same look of disbelief on her face. 'It doesn't matter that she woke me. I don't sleep very much, anyway. Where's the dra . . . Mrs Muffin? She don't like people in the kitchen.'

'She's gone, Louise.' Karen handed her the note she had stuck behind a canister on the counter.

Louise read it, nodded, and said, 'How'd you know who I was?'

Suddenly, the truth seemed important, both for herself, and this girl in front of her. Karen poured out two cups of tea, pushed one toward Louise, passed the cookies. 'Some of the kids mentioned "Lou", but I knew you when I saw you because Brent told me about you. He said you had beauty shining out of you for everyone else to see.'

Louise's eyes flooded but she blinked and cleared them. 'You know him?' she whispered. 'Then where is he? Why hasn't he come home? Are you the nurse he promised us? The special one?'

'I . . . don't know where he is, Louise. I don't know why he hasn't come home. When I came here this afternoon . . .' Good God! Had it only been then? . . . 'I expected to find him here. I'm not sure I'm the nurse he promised you, but I might be. He asked me to come but at first I was afraid and said I couldn't. Then, in a few days, I got over being afraid and just came as soon as I could. He doesn't know I'm here, maybe he won't want me to stay when he does come here, but it seems I have to stay at least until then . . . there's no one else, is there?'

'Why were you scared?'

'Louise, I'd rather not answer that.'

'Don't you like us because we're Indians?'

'That had nothing to do with my being scared. It was a very special thing that I've got over now so it's not important. When I refused to come with Brent, I had no idea

129

that you were Indians and if I had, it would have had no bearing on my decision. I might not be the one he mentioned to you. He could have asked someone else after I refused. What did he say about the one who was coming?'

'He said she would love us simply because we were, not because we deserved to be loved, or were such lovable people, but because she had so much love in her soul that it would just have to spill out. He said she looked like an angel with dark eyes and pale hair that hung and flew and lived all of its own accord and that her mouth had a natural curve of sweetness and she laughed like a mountain stream. He wrote all that in a letter and then he came home for part of a day and all of one night, saying he was going to bring her back with him in a day or so.

'He came back, but he didn't bring her and his face was so sad and mad all at the same time we didn't ask where she was and then he got a message on the radio-phone and went away. He hasn't come back and we don't know where he is.'

'Was Miss Lowe still here the last time he came back?'

'Yes, but two aides were gone and we didn't want to tell him. I was in the office when the call came through and he told me to go out. Ten minutes later he was gone in the speedboat and he hasn't come back. The call he got was from some woman who called him "Brent, darling," and when she started to talk he asked me to go. When he came tearing out of the office he just called out to me, I was in my garden, to tell Miss Lowe and Mrs Muffin he'd be back in a day or so and to hold the fort. I told Miss Lowe that the nurse he had promised us had just called him and she was coming in a day or so. She called the water taxi and left.'

'And that was . . . how long . . . ago?'

'Couple of weeks.'

'And there's been no word from Brent since then?'

'No . . . I've been in the office or around all the time, except for today after Freddy told me you were mean and ugly-looking and that you had told him right off that I couldn't look after the little ones any more, and then I stayed in my garden with them so you couldn't find us. If a call had come through I'd have known . . . unless it was when I wasn't close enough and the dra . . . Mrs Muffin took it.'

'I didn't tell Freddy anything of the sort!'

'I know,' said Louise, 'and he was lying

about how you look.' She yawned, said, 'Goodnight, nurse.'

'Please, Lou . . . call me Karen. I'd really pre . . .'

'Karen?' Louise interrupted, not rudely but excitedly, 'Karen? Then you are Brent's nurse! He said your name was Karen! Oh, wait'll I tell the kids about this in the morning! You won't have any more trouble, Karen, they'll love you because Brent said they would!'

Karen got to her feet too, took the roast from the counter, saw it was cool enough to put in the refrigerator and said slowly, 'No . . . no, Lou. Let's not tell them. You see, Brent was angry when I told him I couldn't come with him and he might not want me to stay. Besides, I'd kind of like it if the kids decided on their own that I was acceptable, not just because Brent wanted them to be nice to me . . .'

SIX

There were times within the next few days that Karen came close to calling 'uncle' and letting Louise tell the kids to be nice to her 'or else', but something kept holding her back, some stubborn little voice inside which insisted that she could, would win out. Among the youngest ones there was little problem. Jill and Tommy, the two 'babies' of the home, there, Louise said, because to have a proper home, a family must have babies, had taken to Karen immediately, crawling into her lap whenever she had time to form one.

The next group above the two three year olds were the five and six year olds, two boys, Bill and Joey, and three girls, Rose, Lily and Flo. Then Julie, the only eight year old of either sex, and a whole room full of boys ranging from nine year old Mike to eleven year old Peter, their two room mates, Grant and Paul, both ten as were Mary, the blind one, and Francie. Both Mary and Francie showed signs of greater friendliness since Karen had begun to make time to read bedtime stories to anyone who cared to listen. Billy, different from just plain Bill, was twelve and his two room mates were thirteen . . . Harry and George, both quiet boys who seemed to be totally indifferent to Karen's presence. The worst hold-outs were, and would be for some time, Karen feared, the three teenage boys; Frankie, after his initial relief over the diaper situation, had reverted to following Freddy's rather belligerent lead. Big Peter, called so to distinguish between him and Peter with asthma, wasn't belligerent, he didn't seem to follow Freddy's lead, he just did not follow . . . anyone . . . or any instruction . . . or any suggestion. Blithely, he went his own way, oblivious to the hurt or hardship he might cause others. He was constantly infuriating Margo who, at fifteen, felt it her business to protect the smaller ones from having their crutches pushed out from under them or their chairs jostled simply because Peter wanted to move from point A to point B. Greta, the one who loved music and longed to dance, was the only one of the older girls who felt that Karen was a complete loss, and argued the point voluably with both Margo and June after they had retired to their room for the night. Karen had heard some of these hot discussions.

Her greatest help and ally, indeed, for the first day or two, her only ally, was Louise, one of the kids . . . and yet not one of them. She had spent the past five years in the home, ever since its inception, but when she had reached eighteen, instead of leaving as she maybe should have, she had stayed . . . She had no official designation, but Karen recognized her worth as a liason between children and staff. It was Louise who began the custom of having teams of children clear the table after each meal, load the dishwasher, put the clean things away and set the table for the next meal. She decided that there was no reason kids in chairs couldn't push a vacuum cleaner, one holding the nozzle, another kicking the machine ahead of him or herself. Others helped with the dusting, with the folding of laundry and with the myriad other chores involved in running such a large place.

The fantastic relief afforded Karen by this help was reflected in the happier attitude of those of the children who could or would enjoy the activities the extra time allowed her to prepare for them. She had a toffee pull in the kitchen one night . . . was it only her second or third night there? . . . and one afternoon took the entire group on an exploration of the boardwalks, or rather they took her!

The paths equipped for the use of wheel-chairs and crutches were extensive, leading into the woods, along the sides of the steep bluffs, bridging gulleys and creeks and eventually leading to a beautiful clearing where the grass was lush and long and the boardwalks criss-crossed, giving access to every corner of the field, but converging in the center where five tall totems stood guard.

Karen craned her neck upward, trying to decipher the faces and figures carved on the massive posts. 'Oh, Margo! Do you know what they mean? Tell me about them. They're fantastic!'

Margo tried: 'The figure on top of this one is a Thunderbird. It's like an eagle . . .' she pointed to the top figure on another pole, '. . . But the eagle is plain, it doesn't have horns . . . I think. You should ask Freddy. He knows it all, can read them the way we read a book, or the way Greta can read music. Freddy!' He looked over disinterestedly at Margo's call.

'Come and tell Karen about the totems.'

He shot her a distainful look. 'She

doesn't care about them. If she does, let her find a book about it.'

Karen sighed softly. She wished Freddy had been willing to instruct her; therein might have lain the key she needed with which to reach him. She knew that if she could win Freddy, half . . . no, most of her troubles would be solved. He caused more problems than any one child deserved to cause through instigating the others to do things. Most susceptible were the nine to thirteen year old boys, but it was not until late on her fourth day with the children that she realized just what a problem Freddy really was . . .

The younger ones were all in bed. The six teenagers . . . older teenagers, that was, from fifteen to seventeen, were playing Monopoly in the living room while Karen read a book beside the snapping fire which glowed through the mesh screen in front of it. It was a quiet, peaceful scene, the soft talk of the kids, the crackling of burning wood, the chatter of an aspen near the window and the distant rush and recession of the surf on the rocks below the house. Karen yawned widely, stretched, and as if her hands moving up and out had been a signal, the lights went off, plunging the room into total darkness.

'Oh — oh,' said Freddy hollowly, 'The plant's quit or the breakers have blown.' There was the sound of crutches moving, of a body bumping into something.

'Sit still,' said Karen. 'I'll find a flashlight.' A soft beam crossed the room, flicked onto her face and off again.

'I have one,' said Freddy, and Karen should have realized then . . . but she was too grateful for the light he brought to her . . . too grateful for his unexpected offer to go with her to show her the location of the breaker-switch panel, to think about the fact that he had a flashlight conveniently to hand.

It was not until later, much later, with the acrid odour of smoke still in her nose and throat, the terror still in her heart and mind that she had time to think, to consider . . .

The breakers had been all right. The trouble must be at the plant, over the hill and in the next bay, to keep the scent of diesel oil and the sound of the engine from disturbing the peace of the home, and it was to the plant that Karen had to go alone. The woods were dark and somewhat scary . . . the track was rough and treacherous . . . and Karen made the return trip much faster than she had the trip out. By then she was furiously, blazingly angry, both with herself for being so easily duped, and with Freddy for having duped her. The lighting plant had been running smoothly and well on more than half a tank of fuel!

As she emerged from the clinging limbs and bushes which hung over the trail and caught sight of the bulk of the house, a small flare in one of the back bedrooms caught her eye. She hurried even more, but the sudden blaze of light which whipped with horrifying rapidity to fill one side of the window sent her flying forward, sobs of terror and desperation coming with her short gasps for breath.

In an instant which lasted for three years she was inside the room pointing an extinguisher at the flaming curtain, eyes taking in the choking, huddled form of Mike in his wheelchair beating at the flames until she snatched him away and smothered the fire in foam. Peter, the asthmatic, lay in rigid terror, his breathing raspy, tears pouring from his face, staring intently at Mike who was as yet unaware that the danger was past. Paul and Grant, eyes tearing from the smoke, were slightly more calm, but Karen knew hysteria was imminent.

She pulled Mike out of the way, jerked the window up, opened the door and shoved Peter's bed out into the hall which was crowded with kids who had come, alerted by the screams Karen had not even heard. 'Open the door,' she snapped at a dim figure outside the beam cast by her flash-light, and wheeled the choking boy out into the dark, cool air of night . . .

Now she lay in her bed with the terror still in her heart, the scent of smoke still clinging to her skin and hair . . . no amount of showering would remove it, just as no amount of telling herself, as she had told the children, that all was well, all were safe, would expunge the scene from her mind.

Karen slipped into a fitful doze, only to jerk awake again, hear again Mike's hysterical voice: 'I was putting a candle in the window so you wouldn't get lost! He told me . . . I figured you'd only see the breakers all up and not know about the master-switch but then I got scared that you wouldn't find your way back from the plant . . .'

That, then explained the inexplicable . . . how Freddy, safely in the living room under Karen's eye, had made the lights go out . . . a joke which might have had horrible consequences!

Karen slept past her normal time of arising, awoke with a headache and a general feeling of heaviness which was not lessened by the morning chorus of arguments and squabbles coming from the different rooms along the corridor. She dressed wearily, just as wearily helped those children who could not help themselves and led the way to the kitchen where, thankfully, Louise had breakfast well underway with the joyous hindrance of two three year olds, neither of whom were severely handicapped and therefore almost as mobile as more normal children.

Karen put the coffee on, knowing she was going to need it, lots of it! to face the day ahead.

After the meal Karen chased the work crew out. 'I'll do the dishes myself,' she said, ushering a group of chairs away from the dishwasher. 'Please kids, I have a headache . . .' Now! Now she could pour out a cup of that coffee that she had made and had not yet had time to drink. She thankfully put her favourite large mug in the centre of the table, took the pot from the stove . . . and set it back down quickly, startled by the loud shriek from the dining room.

The quarrel between Greta and Big Peter mediated to the best of her poor ability, Karen slid through the kitchen doorway again, heading for her coffee, determined that this time, nothing would prevent her having it! She poured it, sniffing the aroma appreciatively, watching the steam rise in little white streamers and lowered her aching limbs onto a chair . . .

'Karen! Karen!' Louise's voice, showing panic, an emotion not normally associated with Louise, Karen knew, sent her flying to the door to meet the girl trying to run with her reeling gait. Her eyes were wide and afraid as she gasped, 'Freddy! Freddy's in the bay! Come quick! Help him!'

Karen flew out of the house, across the wide porch and down the sloping ramp toward the float. He was holding onto a half-submerged crate, black head bobbing up and down, arm waving frantically and Karen yelled, 'Hold on!' as she dove overboard, coming up in full stroke, losing her sandanls as her swift crawl took her toward the boy. She treaded water while she ripped off her shirt, flung an arm of it to him, said loudly, 'Freddy! Grab it! I'll pull you in!' Time later to find out what he was doing in the water!

'Aww. I'm awright!' He sounded totally disgusted with her. 'I c'n swim . . . it's this guy, here.'

Oh, my God! Another one? But which one? Two panicking kids in the water could well drown all of them! She edged closer, peered around the crate to which Freddy clung . . . there, just *inside* the crate, or so it appeared, she could see the other head, sleek, wet, black . . . seal-like . . . oh, Lord! It *was* a seal! 'Freddy! For God's sake take the sleeve of my shirt! The damned seal can swim! Leave him alone!'

For once, he did not sneer. For once, he did not give her a bold, derisive look as he said . . . not 'Nursey', but . . . 'Karen! We gotta help him! He *can't* swim! He's all covered with oil!' There was a tremor in his voice which had nothing to do with his shivering. His eyes were shining, not with meanness, but with . . . tears? Freddy? Tears for an oil-soaked seal?

Karen gave her feet enough of a kick to put her into position to see the small, sleek head, its marble eyes staring imploringly at her, and to see the rainbows of oil circling him in the water of the crate. 'Please, Karen!' he begged. 'Please help him! I know I don't deserve it but honest! I didn't know Mike would light a candle!'

'Can you help me tow the box?' asked Karen.

How does one get an oily, slippery, frightened and angry seal out of a slatted crate and into a large kitchen? One quickly wraps the seal in a shirt which one had taken off in an attempt to save a drowning boy, and when that fails, when sharp teeth and claws on flippers tear through the soft material, one strips off one's jeans and wraps the ungrateful creature in those, carrying the squirming, barking, dangerous burden as quickly as possible to the house, while one's clinging, dripping undies attract much giggling attention!

The giggling attention was short-lived, however, when Karen gently deposited her now ominously still burden on the floor and began to undo the knots she had made when she tied the legs of her jeans around the creature. The last knot came loose with a horrifying jerk and Karen leaped back, shoving wheelchairs out the door in front of her, grabbing kids on crutches and moving them out of harm's way as the snapping, snarling, barking, writhing, jumping seal showed his displeasure at having been rescued!

She slammed the door, the mercifully stout door, behind her and leaned on it, staring with shocked eyes as they all listened to the horrific racket being made in the kitchen. There were clatters and thumps and bangs, rattles, barks and wheezes, and then, a dreadful, frightening silence . . .

Karen edged the door open, slamming it quickly as a sinuous, furious body flung itself toward her, but that brief glimpse had been enough to reveal black streaks of oil cutting figure eights across the floor, smearing the counter and table tops, to show spice cans littering the floor along with canisters emptied of their contents; coffee, flour, sugar, tea mingled on the floor along with one thing which convinced her she had to put a stop to the depredation being done . . . her coffee! Not just the cup she had poured and not drunk, but the whole potful, pooled on the floor with the impudent seal slipping in it as he lunged toward the partly open door.

'I think our kitchen's been hijacked,' she said to the children and was rewarded by loud, too-loud, too-prolonged, laughter, but the tension which had been building, broke. 'We have to think of a way to lure him into the laundry room. There's less damage he can do there, both to himself and the room. Any ideas?'

There were a few . . . Climb in the window and lure him in with a fish? Only one problem, all the fish were in the freezer and the freezer was in the kitchen with the seal! Wait 'til he gets tired and rush him with a blanket? Might have to, but will we have a kitchen left by the time he gets tired? Build a wall of wheelchairs and herd him into the laundry room? Hmmm . . . maybe! . . .

. . . And it worked!

It worked with surprising ease in spite of Karen's fears of nipped feet, of a slippery body double-crossing them and flipping up and over the wall, forcing the children into the laundry room instead. When she slammed the door and leaned against it, her knees shaking, to survey the devastated kitchen, she could hardly believe this was all happening to her. She shook her head slowly from side to side . . . 'The only fun and gaiety are what we make for ourselves . . .' Oh, yes! Oh, yes indeed! We do make fun and gaiety for ourselves!

Greta said, worried, 'What are you going to do now, nurse?'

Karen gave her a weak, crooked grin, 'What am I going to do now? I'm going to have a cup of coffee!'

'Don't you want to put some clothes on first, Karen?' asked Louise.

'No . . . but I would like to have my housecoat.'

'I'll get it, Karen! And then I'll change.'

Karen smiled happily. 'Thanks, Freddy. Thanks a lot!'

While she sipped coffee, happily agreeable to Louise's decree that she not move a muscle, Karen watched her charges clean up the kitchen as best they could but, as Greta put it, using her name for the first time because now Freddy accepted Karen, 'We can't sweep or vacuum, Karen. All that stuff's in the hijacker's room.'

As if on cue, the hijacker began to make strange sounds; sounds like a sick kitten, a distant seagull . . . sounds like a small, frightened, hungry seal, lonely, locked up in a cold, strange room might make. Nearly two dozen black eyes squinted in empathetic pain. Nearly two dozen lower lips were bitten between white teeth. 'Oh, Karen! He's crying!' Nearly two dozen pairs of eyes flew to her face, questioning, expecting her to do something about the fact that a small seal was weeping and alone.

'We're all like that when we first come here,' said Grant sadly.

'Yes,' agreed June. 'We raise the roof and get put in the crying room all by ourselves until we stop screaming and start to cry quietly . . .'

'Then,' chimed in Frankie, 'someone comes to talk to us and feed us and make us start to feel at home.'

Someone? For 'someone' read Karen! Talk to it? Tell it what? Feed it? Feed it what . . . her hands, her feet? Make it feel at home? Good grief! But those almost two dozen pairs of eyes expected her to do just that . . . for the first time in five days she had the oportunity to win the trust of each one of these kids. They were all ready now to accept her, to let her take over. But to take over a furious, oil-soaked seal? Was that part of the bargain, the partnership she had been offered? But it was a bargain, a partnership she had refused, and now must earn if she wanted to stay . . . and oh! how she wanted to stay . . .

She pulled a package of sea-trout from the freezer . . . at least that's what the writing on the wrapping proclaimed them to be, and set them in the sink to thaw.

'We'll have our lunch,' she said, putting off the evil moment, 'and when the hijacker's fish is thawed, I'll go and see him.'

'How you gonna do it, Karen?' That was Joey. Good question, she thought silently while trying to look confident. It seemed easy enough when the trainer in the zoo held up a nice little fish and the seal jumped up and took it neatly, daintily, slipping back into the water to do more tricks, secure in the knowledge that there was a never-ending supply coming his way. 'How you gonna feed him?' repeated Joey.

'I'm going to heave a few fish inside and slam the door quick!'

When the whimpering stopped and Karen at last developed enough courage to push the door open a crack, the seal lay on the floor, sleeping . . . feigning sleep? and of the fish there were no sign. The poor little animal's coat was starred and peaked with the oil clinging to it, the oil which would have eaten away his natural water-proofing and eventually killed him . . . Karen approached warily, conscious of the wall of children behind her, the children who expected her to talk to the seal, make him feel at home now that he had had his turn at raising the roof, crying quietly and then being fed.

She knelt down, gingerly touched the head where it widened into slim shoulders while her other hand held a fish, ready to throw it, as her taut legs were coiled ready to leap back. The little creature opened one glassy eye, looked myopically at her, pushed his head harder against her hand and closed his eye again.

'Oh, you poor little thing,' she crooned, 'you poor, innocent baby. You were so frightened, so bewildered, that's why you tore the kitchen apart. Never mind . . . you're home now, and safe, and we all love you . . . Poor, poor Hijacker . . .' and much more nonsense which pleased her audience a great deal and made Karen feel like an utter idiot until the seal hitched himself closer, leaned against her knees and snored! Then Karen felt good . . . very good!

When, at length, cramped and depleted of words suitable to comfort a seal, Karen rose, Hijacker whimpered again and flippered in her wake while the children watched, wide-eyed and ready to scatter should the occasion warrant it. It followed her out of the kitchen, into the hallway and to the living room, and the kids followed both nurse and seal.

Karen sat in a chair and her seal

flippered his way up into her lap. She sat very still while it burrowed close, slipping into the gap between her leg and the arm of the chair, forcing himself closer until only a small, bewhiskered nose was showing.

'Can I feel him?' whispered Julie, and she was the start of a long line of children, small and large, who wanted to stroke, to touch, to become acquainted with the newest member of the family.

'How are we going to get him clean?' And again Karen asked for ideas.

'Turpentine?'

'Wouldn't that burn him?' Ditto lighter-fluid, although the last was academic; she only had one small can. Butter was suggested, discarded. Tomato juice? No, that was for taking skunk odour out of dogs' and cats' fur. Soap and water? Maybe, but wouldn't the water have to be too hot before it'd do any good?

After much discussion Karen remembered a day when she had got sticky, gooey tar from a newly done road all over her tires and shoes. A garage mechanic had suggested she use some cola, and it had worked beautifully. But was there any of it here?

'Sure, three cases left over from some a

store sent us at Christmas,' said Margo. 'We didn't drink it all and Brent said we'd better save it for a special occasion in case we didn't get a donation like that again.'

Neither Karen nor any of the children, and certainly not Hijacker had ever seen a bathtub with three cases of pop poured into it! He frolicked, cavorted, splashed and snorted until Karen and her phalanx of 'helpers' were brown and sticky, the walls and floor were brown and sticky and slowly the oil was worked out of the seal's hair. After a final rinse he looked more like a seal than an old fur coat from a garbage dump, and he flippered quite happily after Karen and her retinue, feeling much more at home.

SEVEN

Overnight Karen learned one great lesson: Hijacker was very much at home, so much in fact, that having enjoyed wrecking the kitchen the previous day, he decided the entire house needed to be rearranged, and chose to start in one of the bathrooms. Karen awoke to a terrible clatter and rushed out to see what was causing it, skidding to a halt with a groan, 'Oh, Hijacker!' when she found him deep in one of the bathtubs playing catch with a can of scouring powder. A fine coating of it covered him as well as the floor, and a dust of it floated in the air, making him sneeze and cough, disturbing even more of it. He had torn towels from the rails, tossed bars of soap here and there and even managed to open one of the toilet cubicles; streamers of paper festooned the room.

He laughed at her as she stood, hands on hips, staring down at him slithering across the gritty tub, and in spite of herself, Karen laughed back, turning on the shower to cleanse him. This was exactly the answer to his prayers and he grinned even more impudently, his entire demeanor saying, 'See? It just takes a little training and a seal can have a person doing the right trick on command every time!'

When the last of the powder had gurgled down the drain Karen left the seal playing under a trickle of water and began to clean up but, tiring of the shower after a few minutes, Hijacker considered it necessary to lend a hand . . . or at least a flipper.

He flopped out of the tub and landed in the pile of towels she had gathered up, shaking them villianously to teach them to stay off the floor and not make work for Karen. The towels released another cloud of powder and she scooped both cloth and seal up quickly to carry them to the laundry room. When she returned, it was just in time to hear an outraged feminine voice roaring, 'Boy! Look at the mess those boys made! Wow! Wait'll Karen sees this! Bet she won't talk about being tolerant of other's mis . . .'

'This was no mistake,' said Karen from the doorway. 'This was deliberate sabotage by one seal. Sorry girls. The tubs'll be ready for you in a few minutes. Anyway, what are you doing up so early?'

Margo clearly thought Karen's sanity

was in doubt. 'Karen! It's the *seventh!*'

Not understanding the significance of the date, Karen said, 'So?'

'So it's the day Mr Edmund comes!'

'Mr Edmund? Who's he?' Oh, no, thought the hard-pressed nurse, if he's an inspector of some sort, I'll hide! For she had just noticed that Hijacker, while knowing tubs were for getting wet in, had other ideas . . . wrong ones . . . of their use as well! All I need is someone like that when I have a seal which needs to be housebroken!

'He's our teacher! We got to go to school, you know!'

'I . . . never thought about it, really, I guess. But no one's ever mentioned him to me!'

'Didn't we? Well, we were on vacation. But he always comes on the seventh . . . unless he's forgotten, too . . .' Margo's mouth drooped and Karen gave her a swift hug, knowing reassurances were in order.

'Of course he hasn't! And neither has Brent! I know it! He loves you all and he *will* come back. I promise!'

'How do you know? Karen, you don't even know Brent!'

'I know him very well just from having heard you kids talk about him and I know he wouldn't disappoint you like this unless

155

he honestly couldn't help it. Now you just hold on and be patient and he'll show up whenever he can.'

Margo wrapped thin arms around Karen's neck and held her tightly for a moment. 'Oh, Karen! I'm so glad we got you! You sounded just like Brent last night when you told Big Peter that no one was going to be sent away for having played a practical joke that might have hurt people. Poor Mike . . . he thought we all hated him, just because of what Pete said.' Her eyes glowed. 'But wasn't it great when Freddy told us all it was his fault, not Mike's?' She lowered her lamp-bright eyes, looked at her hands and said, 'I kinda like Freddy, you know, Karen,' and her voice trembled, as only the voice of a girl feeling the first pangs of puppy-love, can.

Gently Karen said, 'I kind of like Freddy, too. He's got to be a pretty nice person inside to ask someone he thought he hated for help to save a seal that was going to die.'

Greta, by this time, had finished rinsing out the tub she wanted to use and heard the last bit. 'Freddy didn't really hate you, Karen, he just didn't want to like you because you weren't the one Brent promised us.' She frowned thoughtfully, 'Hey, how

156

did you get to come here, anyway?'

Karen drew in a long breath to give herself a moment for frantic thought. 'Well . . . you know the home is run by a foundation . . . and I talked to Mr Hobbs who . . . administers it,' she said ambiguously. It wasn't really a lie, and it did seem to satisfy the girls for no more was said on the subject as Karen helped Greta into a tub and then in turn, the others, by which time it was the moment to start breakfast and get another day rolling.

She was walking slowly back from a trek with the kids out into the forest where they had spent some time on a bridge over a creek watching the fish dart to and fro, looking at the ferns and mosses along the bank, Karen being given a spot of education as the children told her what each species of flora was, when Louise came rushing out to meet her, her face alive with an inner light.

'Karen! Karen! I have to talk to you . . . in private!'

They went into Lou's own little garden through the long glass door which let into the wilderness of ferns and phlox and chrysanthemums, of marigolds and cosmos, growing tangled and beautiful among the small wild shrubs, and sat on a bench made from slabs of wood perched on blocks cut from a tree trunk.

Louise could hardly contain herself, blurting out, as she sat down, 'He does know you're here! He called Karen, Brent called and he's been in an accident, that's why he didn't come home! He asked me how we liked the nurse he sent us in his place and I said that we all love you and you were out with the kids right now so he couldn't talk to you!' She sucked in a deep breath and went on, 'I told him I was the only one who knew he had sent you because you wanted the kids to like you for your own sake and he said, Good for her. I should have told her to do that myself, but I didn't think of it; I was too banged up.'

Karen had been trying to break in, but now that Louise was silent, she could barely force the words from her horribly dry mouth. 'What happened? How badly hurt is he?'

Louise looked at her quickly, touched her hand. 'Karen! You're freezing! And you're so white! He's all right. He and a truck collided and he got a concussion and a broken leg. He had to stay in the hospital until he stopped getting dizzy so he wouldn't fall and break his leg again . . . he said.' She looked confused and then said slowly, 'But he told me . . . he asked *his* nurse to come . . . after . . . when he knew he wouldn't be back . . . right away.' Her eyes widened as she realized what Karen had known right from the beginning: Karen could not be the nurse Brent had just been discussing with Lou! And in that case, who was that nurse? Where?

'Did either of you mention a name when you were talking about the nurse?'

Louise thought for a minute or two. 'No,' she whispered, shaking her head. 'He just asked me if we liked the nurse he had sent us and I said yes and we went on talking about "her" and "she" . . . . But where is she? He got hurt the day he left here and he said he asked her right away to . . .'

The sound of an approaching sea-plane cut across her words. 'Maybe . . . ?'

'No,' said Louise, with finality. 'That'll be the teacher. You'd better go and meet him.'

'Well come with me! Make the introductions and all that!'

'No!' It was almost a yelp. 'No . . . I . . . my hips are aching, Karen. I don't want to move.'

'Oh, Lou! You shouldn't have come running out to meet me! Come and lie down and I'll give you a rub.'

'No. The teacher'll expect to be met.'

Now what? thought Karen, walking out through Louise's room and to the front of the house in time to see the plane taxi across the bay and take off toward the mountains on the other shore, while a stocky man, too distant for her to make out any details, gathered up a load of suitcases and headed up the ramp, his face raised to the house . . . eagerly, it seemed.

A herd of children coasted and thudded along the porch, separating around her as though she were an obstacle to be bypassed, and rushed toward the long, sloping ramp and the man, calling, yelling, laughing, 'Mr Edmund! Mr Edmund! Hi, how are you? Have a nice summer? Didja bring the things you said you would?'

Karen felt a lump grow in her throat as the man dropped his bags and waded among the children, hugging, patting, giving out warm words, smiles, leaving out not one child, having something special to say to each one, even though it was unlikely his words were understood in the clamour of voices.

The children convoyed him up the ramp

to where Karen stood. She held out her hand and smiled, 'Hi, Mr Edmund. I'm Karen Jamison . . . at the moment, chief keeper of this zoo. Looks as though you're being very warmly welcomed, but may I add my own?'

He gave her a friendly, appraising glance. 'You most certainly may! And may I say that you're a welcome surprise? I was sure I'd find the dragon and the witch still in firm position. Where's the boss?'

'Which one's the boss? The dragon . . . or the witch?'

He gave her a charming grin which lighted up his rather deep-set eyes. 'Brent, of course! Neither of those two qualify to boss a flea circus!'

Karen frowned slightly, casting a meaningful glance at the 'little pitchers' around them. He laughed, patted a few heads and shoulders. 'Oh, don't worry about that. We understand each other, don't we, kids? That's one of the first things I gleaned from the babble; both the dragon and the witch were gone and Karen was here. What did you do? Drown 'em?'

Karen led the way indoors, laughing. 'Miss Lowe was gone when I arrived and Mrs Muffin left soon after. But you're no help at all, Mr Edmund, in my attempts at teaching tolerance.'

'Now you're trying to get on the good side of the teacher,' he accused. 'Talking in alliteration. Somebody told you I'm a fan of Swinburn!'

'What's alliteration?' Karen asked with mock ignorance. 'And isn't Swinburn the world tiddly-winks champion?'

He laughed. 'My Lit professor would have loved you. Such a vacuum to be filled with knowledge!' Then, sobering. 'But if the dragon's gone, who's been doing the cooking and whatever?'

'I have.'

'You? Oh. I thought, I don't know why, but I thought you were a nurse.' He hesitated. 'Not that you look like one in those shorts and that thing . . . but you look even less like a housekeeper!'

'This thing . . . happens to be a halter-top and unfortunately for both your digestion and the sake of your health, I'm both housekeeper and nurse.'

He pursed his lips and shook his head, but before he could comment, Karen suggested that he get his unpacking done so he could be ready for dinner in a hour and a half.

Much later, the two adults sat on the porch watching the approaching night darken the waters of the inlet and fill the bay with a mysterious light. Don, as he asked Karen to call him, sighed. 'Lord! Is it ever good to be home!'

'Peace . . . good, isn't it?' said Karen. 'How come you're the teacher here? Seems more like a job for a woman . . . or am I being too anti-lib, slotting jobs by sex?'

'Not really . . . there are some that . . . but until I came two years ago, there'd been trouble keeping women here. Too isolated, for one thing, and as you may know, these kids can be difficult!'

'Oh! Do I know!' Under his sympathetic, understanding questioning, Karen found herself giving a full account of the happenings since her arrival and, without her knowing quite how, the immediate events leading up to it.

'So he finally took a vacation,' said Don. 'He needed it. And he met you, asked you to come here and you refused. When you changed your mind, you arrived here and found him gone and the dragon in charge, so you threw her out.' He grinned his infectious grin. 'Oh, I know, not really! You don't look like St George, but then, you don't look like a seal-trainer, either!'

'Nor a nurse, nor a housekeeper,' she reminded him. 'And you look more like a high-school kid than you do a teacher!'

'Meaning, how old am I?'

'A clever high school kid,' Karen smiled, making no apology for having asked, even in her round-about way.

'I'm twenty six, university educated and spent the summer taking a course in the care, feeding and education of Indian kids . . . this is called "Intercultural Education". It's a valuable program, one every teacher of Indian children should have if our culture isn't to die out.' He must have seen her momentary surprise, for he quirked his quick smile at her, saying, 'Oh, yes, I said "our" and that's what I meant.

'My grandmother on one side was a full Nootka married to a Nootka-Portugese half-breed. On the other side was a grandmother of Kwakiutl and English married to a 'Scandihoovian'. I get the curls from the Portugese line, the brown eyes from any of them maybe, and the pale-face look from the white portions of my blood. I'm a real mish-mosh, Karen, but I think of myself as a Nootka. Did you know that it was with my ancestors that Captain Cook first met here? Notably, Maquinna, the great chief.'

Karen did not know, but was willing to be informed, and when dark had long since fallen, it was with regret that she went to help the older children to bed.

The next day was Sunday and Karen saw Don only at mealtimes; he was busy getting the school ready in one of the outbuildings Karen had never explored. In the evening he was still hard at it, but refused her offer of help. 'Lady, you have enough to do! If you're done all your chores, go and sit down for half an hour. I've never seen such a glutton for punishment. But,' he added somewhat diffidently, 'If you could spare one of the older girls . . . Louise, for instance, I could use some help with this cataloguing.'

'Sure! I'll send her right in.'

Well, mused Karen much later, I *thought* I'd send her right in! What in the world had come over Louise . . . her good, obliging, helpful Louise? If it hadn't been for Margo, Karen would have gone back to the school-room and offered her aid once more, but Margo, bless her generous heart, had swiftly volunteered when Louise had so vehemently stated that she was far too busy. With what? Karen asked herself, looking down at the two little ones on her lap with the seal, the latter shifting now and then as if reluctant to go on sharing.

Billy leaned against Karen on the left,

humming quietly. Julie shrilled her high-pitched tones into Karen's right ear as they, along with the others, sang the hymn Greta was playing on the piano. She moved the little girl out by her foot-stool, saying quietly, 'There, now I can hear you with both ears. So much better,' and raised her voice in song with the surrounding children, all present this evening with the exception of Margo and the suddenly recalcitrant Louise.

They looked so beautiful, so peaceful as they sang the ancient hymns taught to their forefathers by the missionaries who had come to this coast, and then, as a strange piece of music began, the children chanted a poignantly haunting song in a language alien to Karen. When it was over and the voices had slowly faded in harmony, she rubbed at the goose-bumps on her arms and said, 'What was that? It was lovely!'

'The Lord's prayer in Chinook,' said Greta.

Frankie volunteered: 'Chinook was a trade language, a mixture of a lot of words from a lot of tongues and dialects, with some English and French, too. None of the Indians spoke each other's special languages very well, and the fur-traders didn't speak any of them so they came up with a common language they could use for trading.' He would have gone on, and Karen was interested, but the clamouring of the younger children was loud.

'We want to sing! Play, Greta, 'cause we have go to bed early . . . school tomorrow!' For the five and six year olds, this was a big thing; the six year olds were entering grade one, and the fives, kindergarten, all run by the capable Mr Edmund.

To Karen's disappointment, the children knew only two more native songs, and then Greta began to play a hymn which made Karen's muscle's go taut. She fought the stiffness, tried to force herself to sing, concentrated hard on the sweetly solemn faces of these children whom she had grown to love, but the memories were too strong, even with the warming, filling presence of these 'jewels' and the image of her own 'precious jewel' flooded over her as she sang:

'Like the stars of the morning,
His bright crown adorning,
They will shine in their beauty
Bright gems for . . .'

and her voice cracked, broke. She buried her

face against Tommy's small back and let the tears flow.

The piano stopped with a clashing discord and a number of voices cried out, 'Karen!'

Slowly she forced herself to regain control and raised her head to look at the concerned, loving faces staring aghast at her. What have we done? they seemed to be asking. Have we hurt you? Why are you crying? You're our strong one!

Karen wiped her eyes with the back of her hand, forced a tremulous smile which did little to ease the tension in the faces before her. She tried to pass her emotion off as just one of those suddenly blue moods, but they weren't buying it. With disconcerting directness Julie said, 'It was that hymn. It's a special one to us . . . our favourite. Don't you like it?'

All the eyes so steady on her demanded an answer and Karen might have tried to prevaricate again, but suddenly she knew that since she had asked these children to trust her, to rely on her and learn to love her, in all conscience, she could not offer them a lesser commitment. She owed them the truth. 'That hymn was played at the funeral of my daughter who died when she was two. It brought back sad memories, is all. Please play it again, Greta, and we'll all sing.'

'No,' said Mary. 'It's not my favourite anymore. I don't like it. We can't have a special hymn that makes you sad. If that one was played at our sister's funeral then it'll make us sad, too. Right, Julie?'

'Your sister . . . ?'

'If she was your little girl, that one what died, then she's our sister . . . you're sort of our mother.'

Karen bit her lip hard, blinked and tried to quell the instant spurt of fresh tears to her eyes, but in a second she was roaring, along with the older children, with laughter, when Joey piped up. 'A new special hymn? Sure! How 'bout "Yellow Submarine"?'

Karen towed a string of children off to the bedroom wing, marching to the loud strains of 'We all live in a yellow submarine . . .'

How quiet it was the next morning with all but two of the children in class! Louise had the two tinies with her in her garden. She was spending a great deal of time there, reflected Karen, perplexedly. Ever since Brent's phone-call, it seemed, Louise had withdrawn into herself, hiding away, coming out only when she really had to, and then, only in the line of duty.

The seal scrambled around Karen's feet, begging for attention. She stooped and scratched his belly, listening to the lonely silence, and then turned up the volume on the radio, to drown it out with the sound of a brass band. When the seal was more or less satisfied, she began to cut up the remains of Sunday's turkey for hash, and when Hijacker began to beg, she dropped a couple of fish on the floor to keep him occupied while she got on with her work.

The door opened suddenly, but was not closed. Without turning, Karen said to Louise, 'Hey! Shut that door! I don't want Hijacker escaping again!' Because the radio was loud, she had spoken quite loudly, even sharply, it may have been said.

'I beg your pardon?' came the reply in a high, haughty tone which set Karen spinning to see who had spoken, but instead, she slipped on a piece of fish the seal had missed, and fell smack on her jean-clad bottom beside Hijacker who leapt joyously atop her, certain she had dropped in to play.

She scrambled to her feet, staring, goggling, and when the woman spoke again, saying, 'What is that . . . fish! . . . doing in here?' she had still not recovered.

She sucked in a long breath, kicked the fish toward the seal who gobbled it up and then belched as indelicately as only he . . . or Freddy . . . could. 'There!' said Karen in minor triumph, 'it's gone now. Who are you?'

'It was not to *that* fish I was referring,' snapped the woman, ignoring Karen's question, 'but to *that* one!' pointing a perfectly manicured finger at Hijacker.

'Oh, he's not a fish,' said Karen inanely. 'He's a seal.'

'My dear young woman! I am perfectly aware of what it is and if I choose to call a seal a fish, it is not your place to correct me! Why is it in this kitchen?'

'Because he makes too much mess in the bedrooms,' explained Karen, asking again. 'Who are you?' although she knew quite well that this must be the tardy nurse sent by Brent. She stared at the woman, from the tips of her very white shoes, up the length of slim, white-stockinged legs to the hem of the pristine white dress just visible where the royal-blue cape had parted to reveal it and a red satin lining, to the dark sweep of hair under the royal blue cap

171

which would have done justice to Christian Dior, and, last, into the eyes as blue as the cape and as cold and hard as Arctic ice.

'I,' said the woman, 'am Miss Steves. And you . . . are . . . Mrs Muffin?' That she found this hardly credible, was obvious.

'No, Miss Steves. Mrs Muffin has gone. I am . . .'

'I see. One of the aides. Well, Miss, I'm here to take over and before we go any further, I wish you to know that I will not tolerate a member of my staff wearing . . . jeans . . .' an elegant nose wrinkled distainfully . . . 'in duty hours. You will be in my office in exactly half an hour ready with an explanation of why there is a seal in the kitchen of this hospital and,' she paused meaningfully, raking Karen with a disgusted glance, 'in full and proper uniform!'

In precisely half an hour Karen tapped gently on the door of what had suddenly become 'Miss Steves's office', and was graciously bade to enter.

'You wanted to see me, Miss Steves?'

Oh! the unholy joy at seeing that cool composure torn asunder! Oh! the glee when the carefully controlled mouth gaped a good half-inch, and Oh! the deep, pervading sense of pleasurable one-up-manship when the calm, well-modulated voice did not materialize and Miss Steves croaked, 'What?' at the sight of Karen dressed in her white shoes and stockings, her white uniform dress and cap with the black band, pinned prominently to which was the twinkling Star of Honour, given only to one nurse in the combined graduating classes of the four major hospitals whose students competed for the top position every year.

'I said, "You wanted to see me?",' repeated Karen kindly, as if she truly believed the other nurse had not heard her the first time. 'Well,' her smile might have been called impudent, 'here I am!'

Miss Steves, Karen reluctantly admitted, did regain her composure quite rapidly. 'Sit down, please, nurse . . . Miss Lowe, I presume?'

Karen bit back the impulse to say, 'No, Dr Livingstone,' and substituted, 'No, Mrs Jamison. Karen Jamison.'

Did the quickly repaired composure slip a fraction? It was hard to be sure, for in the next instant Miss Steves gave a small, tinkling laugh before saying, 'Oh, no! Not really! The little widow? But my dear, whatever are *you* doing here?'

She folded her beautiful hands in front of her and leaned forward smilingly, inviting a confidence. Karen was unable to speak. 'The little widow'? Brent had spoken about her . . . like that? to this woman? Miss Steves laughed lightly again. 'Don't look so surprised, my dear! Of course I know all about you. Brent and I have known each other for years, and he told me about a young widow he'd taken pity on while on vacation, one Karen Jamison, and had offered her a job. He was so sorry for you my dear, having lost your husband and all, and thought you might like to try something a little different just until I was free to come here. I thought he told me you'd refused, had become a little . . . disturbed . . . at the thought of working with Indian children, so I must confess myself surprised at finding you here, but not as surprised as Brent will be!'

She paused, examined her fingernails minutely, as if seeking possible dust under their immaculate edges, and then said, looking obliquely at Karen, 'Poor Brent, he did feel badly about making you hysterical. He's like that, you know, taking the troubles of even the most casual acquaintances on his shoulders. I've told him and told him that even a psychologist has to take a rest now and then and can't spend his holiday trying to put broken widows back together simply because he feels it his professional duty. However,' she sat up straighter and smiled, a flashing of white teeth, 'I'm sure he'll be pleased to know that his own special brand of therapy worked. Did he tell you, my dear, that before he came here to look after the home, most of his women patients fell madly in love with him? That was one of the reasons he wanted this place so badly. After a while, he couldn't laugh about it any more . . . but I think he's learning to again.

'But now to business. I'm sure you'll realize that Brent intended me to be in charge, my dear, until he comes back, and for some time after he arrives, as he won't really be mobile right away. I hope we'll get along well, each within our own little sphere of influence. It would be so difficult for Brent if we didn't,' she smiled. 'And I feel so responsible for his accident. If I hadn't called him he wouldn't have been driving so fast and none of this would have happened.'

'When . . . when is he arriving?' Karen could hardly believe that that voice was hers!

'In a week or so . . . Oh, don't look so worried! I'll put in a good word for you if he's angry with you for having changed your mind. Tell me, why did you?'

'A challenge was issued. I accepted it, if somewhat belatedly, because I don't care to be called a coward, even by a casual acquaintance. I hope you'll excuse me, Miss Steves, I have to prepare lunch. It'll be late as it is.'

'Of course, my dear,' graciously, smiling with her head on one side. 'And now that I'm aware that we're sisters by profession, I insist you call me Melissa and hope that you'll forgive me for my earlier error. Your dress is entirely up to you, so change into something else, if you wish.'

Karen walked slowly back to the kitchen wishing desperately she *could* change into something else: a bird, so she could fly away! A deer, so she could escape fleetly through the forest! A rock in the bay so she could not feel . . .

EIGHT

'Karen!' She turned slowly, stiffening as she heard Melissa's sharp tone behind her, and set a stack of warm, folded sheets atop the drier. She said nothing, only waiting.

'I will not tolerate any interference in my handling of the children. When I said that I was sure we could get along, each in our own sphere of influence, I did not mean that you were to go on enforcing your own petty little rules on those poor children, especially if it means denying them a treat of my offering. The unforgivable way in which you attacked me before lunch will not be repeated! I hope I make myself quite clear.'

'Oh, yes. Extremely clear, Melissa, if by an "attack" you mean when I told you that I did not want the kids to have chocolate bars immediately before lunch.'

'That is exactly what I meant. You, my dear Karen, do not "tell" me anything! It is your place to *be* told. Just as it is your place to continue to act as housekeeper for as long as is necessary, and to help me with the children when, and only when, I request your help. As I must do now.' That it was distasteful to her to have to do so was clear. What had happened to their being 'sisters by profession'? Karen wondered bleakly.

'The records,' said Melissa, 'are in deplorable order. There have been no proper entries made in the case histories in the past three weeks, a thing which must be rectified at once. Just as soon as you have finished in here, you will report to the office.'

She swept out, leaving Karen to wonder how she was to find time to change all those beds and still get dinner on the table at a decent hour if she had to spend the afternoon bringing the case histories up to date. As she slowly stacked the linen away, putting off the time when she had to report to the office, she let her mind flash back to the scene when the primary children had come roaring out of class, excited, proud and ready to share their new experiences with her.

Joey had got to her first, waving a colourful paper and calling, 'Look! Look what I made! It's for . . .' His voice had died away, his eyes opened wide and Karen turned to see Melissa coming down the hall in full sail, smiling sweetly.

'Oh, you darlings!' she gushed, grabbing Joey's paper and poring over it. 'Why, this is wonderful! You must be Billy. I'm Aunt Melissa. May I have this to hang in my room?'

'I'm Joey. That's for Karen.'

'For Karen?' The high, tinkling laugh rang out. 'But darling, she's far too busy to care about things like this. She'd never have time to look at it! And if you're Joey, then this must be Billy. Hello, dear. Will you give Auntie Melissa a kiss? No? I'll give you a candy for one!' she smiled archly at Bill and he backed away, his crutches squeaking on the floor. Melissa turned next to a group of little girls.

'Are you Flo? I've heard so much about you from your dear Uncle Brent! And you . . . why, you must be Mary!' She bent and put her face close to Mary, lifting the child's hands to her cheeks. 'Can you "see" what I look like, darling, with your fingers? Tell me, do you think I'm pretty?'

'I think you got "runkles" by your eyes,' said Mary with the devastating candour of childhood.

Was the tinkling laugh just a shade brassy? 'Darling! Those are called "laugh lines".'

At that moment Louise and the two tinies came around the corner and Melissa dove at the two babies. 'Oh, our dear little Tommy and Jill. And you must be Louise. Brent has told me what a marvellous help you are to him, Louise. How glad I am to meet you at last! Tommy, come here,' and she scooped him into her arms. Tommy, who did not care to be scooped, especially by a stranger, opened his mouth and bellowed, twisting away and hiding his face in Louise's knees.

Melissa had the good sense to approach Jill more warily and squatted in front of her saying, 'Hello, little one. My, you have pretty hair.' When Jill would have followed Tommy's lead and roared, her open mouth was quite effectively plugged by a large piece of chocolate which materialized seemingly by slight of hand and was popped onto her tongue. Tommy, between howls, heard the magic sound of rustling candy wrappers and turned his eyes to Jill's working jaws. A chocolate bar was slipped into his hot little hand.

'Come along, darlings,' carolled Melissa, leading the way to the dining room, distributing candy bars as she went, and like sheep, the kids followed, whispering, chattering, muttering, and the one phrase which came clearly to Karen's ears was repeated over and over: 'Brent's nurse!'

Karen flung up her head, the light of battle in her eyes and went down the hall through the trail of candy wrappers. 'Excuse me, Melissa, but I don't want the kids to have chocolate just before a meal.' She smiled as she spoke, and then turned to the children, 'Kids, please put your candy beside your plates and save it for later. You know the rules.'

The few chocolate bars or portions thereof were reluctantly laid down while a battery of pained, soulful, injured eyes turned to Karen, pleadingly. She remained firm, but Bill, his eyes on Melissa who was watching Karen, lifted his half-eaten bar toward his mouth. 'Bill, you heard me. Put it down.'

'Go ahead, darling,' crooned Melissa. 'What Karen doesn't know is that your dear Uncle Brent asked me to give you that candy with his love. Now wasn't that nice of him? Go on, my loves, have your little treat. Never mind what mean old Karen says!'

Those greedy little hands and greedy little mouths worked rapidly in concert while Melissa smiled in triumph at 'mean old Karen' until the door opened and the older children came in to stare as had the little ones, at the stranger.

'Oh, the rest of the family. Karen, introduce me to these lovely young people.' Gone was the gushing, too-sweet tone; it was replaced by what sounded like genuine pleasure. Barely able to articulate, Karen complied.

'Oh, but my dears!' How pained Melissa was! 'You mustn't call me Miss Steves! Brent, himself, when he asked me to come said you must call me Aunt Melissa, or if you prefer, just Melissa.' She let a little laugh tinkle again and said, 'I'm afraid Karen's a little annoyed with me for giving the smaller ones candy, but I'm sure even she won't object to big, husky people like you having some.' She smiled around at them, her eyes meeting those of each child for a tender moment before moving on to the next. Unerringly she spotted what might be a problem, and cut it out with no trouble at all.

'My!' she said, her white hand just fluttering over Freddy's shoulder. 'Just look at your wonderful build! You must come from a race of supermen. It would take a man like you to build a dugout, carve a totem or hunt the deadly killer whale! You'll have to tell me all about your people one day when we have a little time just for ourselves.' She gave him an intimate little smile to which he responded by almost grovelling and accepted his chocolate bar with a fatuous grin.

'Well?' she swung to address Karen sharply. 'Is lunch ready? I'm sure we're all ready for it!'

Karen shook herself, smoothed out the last sheet on the stack and went to knock on the door to the office for the second time that day.

'Ah, Karen . . . sit down. We must go through these files, one by one, and you tell me each little item you can remember observing since you arrived.' Her tone implied doubt that Karen's powers of observation were likely to be of much value, but one must work with what one has . . .

'First, Margo. How, exactly, did she react to your arrival? How has her health been, what difficulties is she having, has she complained of any pain or discomfort, what is your opinion of . . .' And so it went, case by case, Melissa taking copious notes until everything was as up to date as possible.

'Now,' she said, folding her hands and leaning over them toward Karen. 'About that fire you unfortunately allowed to happen. Brent will, of course, have to know about it. It will be in the day book. I think, therefore, considering our special . . .' she smiled gently . . . 'relationship, it would be best for him to think I were here when it happened.'

'How will he be able to think that? You weren't!'

'Brent won't need to know that. As far as he'll be concerned, I arrived just the day after his accident, and when you came, I asked you to stay because our housekeeper had just left and I needed help. It will be much better for everyone that way, as you, being here illegitimately, so to speak, cannot possibly take responsibility for anything. Oh, I admit it was good of you to step into the breach, but you must remember you are here uninvited. You could just as easily contacted the Graham Foundation, explained the situation and had them send out a responsible party to take over.

'The fact that you did not puts Brent in an impossible position. He is responsible for the safety and well-being of the children and if it were known that, even inadvertently, he had allowed an unapproved person to have complete charge and during the time of her charge, a potentially dangerous situation had developed, it could go very hard on him indeed. So, on paper, at least, it will appear that I was here when the fire occured; that way, everyone's covered. To keep things correct, I will make all the entries in the cards and sign them just as if I had been here as, of course, I intended to be.'

'But you were unavoidably detained?' Karen did not even try to keep the irony from her tone.

Melissa's nostrils flared fractionally as her eyes sharpened and narrowed and her mouth tightened. 'Exactly! I'm sure you have plenty to do, so you may be excused.' Don, who had wondered at Karen's failure to appear at lunch in the dining room, was even more concerned when both she and Louise were missing at dinner time. He stayed with Melissa and the children for just as long as politeness demanded and then went to the kitchen.

'What's with you two?' he asked. 'Too good for the rest of us?'

'Not good enough!' snapped Louise, still smarting from being told that auxilliary staff would no longer be dining with the 'family'.

Don hauled out a chair and sat close beside her, tapping her hand sharply with his fingers. 'Now cut that out! You're as good as anyone else and I won't have you demeaning one of my favourite people like that.'

Louise's face crumpled as her chair was scraped back and she rushed unevenly from the room, slamming the door. 'What did I do? What did I say?' asked Don, staring at Karen who shrugged unhappily.

She couldn't tell him what she believed to be true; that Louise was in love with him! Lou hadn't come right out and said so, but she had started asking about operations to improve the shape of her mouth, to repair her hips, and this, coming from a girl who had heretofore refused to even discuss the possibility of further operations, was cause for suspicion, especially coupled with little comments about 'Brent's nurse' being just as enchanting to the teacher as she was to his older students.

'He never treated you like that,' she had complained. 'He didn't fall all over himself to pull out your chair! He didn't keep his eyes on your face the whole time you were talking and you're a whole lot prettier than she is! He's just as stupid as Freddy!'

'But Lou! I don't mind Don's treating me like a friend! I wouldn't have it any other way!'

'I know! But I mind!'

'I thought you didn't even like the teacher, Lou.'

'I don't!' was the indignant protest, too indignant, Karen thought suddenly. 'I don't like him at all, but it makes me mad to see him in there with her, smirking at everything she says while you have to eat out in the kitchen so the kids will have a "greater sense of family"! One mother figure, one father figure! What's going to happen when Brent comes back? Will Mr Edmund have to eat in here with us?'

'Let's wait and see . . .'

But Karen couldn't tell Don any of this, so she just shrugged, and in time he went away.

The next two days saw the situation growing worse and worse from Karen's point of view and she feared that her constantly suppressed fury would give her ulcers. But it wasn't until Wednesday evening that it all really blew out of handling size and she was ready to swim out the inlet if that were the only way to leave.

She found Margo alone in the dining room, sniffling as she cleared the table without the help of Freddy, who was supposed to be her partner that night. Karen asked where the boy was.

'He's a direct descendant of Haida chiefs and they don't have to do dishes,' she sneered angrily, banging a stack of plates onto the cart. 'He's gone to tell Melissa all about the totems in the park!'

She came upon them quietly in her sneakers, Big Peter, Frankie, Melissa and Freddy, the latter saying, 'That one at the top is the Thunderbird, the god of the skies. He has a killer whale in his claws. Killer whale is the spirit of the deepest ocean and an enemy of Thunderbird. Below them is the grizzly bear, standing for power, and then comes the wolf, the smart and crafty spirit of the lands. The raven,' he pointed to an enormous beak and evil looking eyes, 'is the god of creation.' He stopped and smiled into Melissa's eyes. He seemed to be finished and Karen stepped forward.

'That was interesting, Freddy. Now would you please come home and help Margo? You must have forgotten you were on duty with her this evening.'

'Melissa said I don't have to,' he said sullenly. 'That's girls' work.'

'That's right.' Melissa staunchly supported Freddy's stand. 'I don't think it's at all fitting for sons of chiefs to be doing dishes or other housework they tell me you've been forcing them to do. Things have changed, Karen, now that there are two nurses and the children are in school all day. I can understand your having needed help before, but it's no longer necessary now that I've taken over so many of your jobs.'

Such as? Karen longed to snap, but she knew she was beaten. The boys, when Melissa started her even-toned explanation had stood watching, waiting impassively for her to dispose of this nuisance so they could get back to an occupation more befitting the 'sons of chiefs'! If Karen had said one word, it would have been her whom the boys saw to be in the wrong, not Melissa, who was always careful to make good sense and speak politely to Karen when in the presence of the children.

Karen left, telling herself that this was the end, she was going to leave, there was no need for her to stay here! As she trod along the boards her heels angrily said, 'Running away, running away, running away!' a bitter memory of a mocking voice, and she changed her pace to hear her heels ring out: 'Cow . . . ard, cow . . . ard, cow . . . ard!'

She was curled in her favourite chair with the seal and the little ones on her lap, a circle of others around her listening to the story she was reading when Melissa came in, took one glance at the tableau, and said, 'Karen . . . do you really think the living room is the place for the seal? I worry about all the strange germs he might be giving to the children. I'd like him taken back to the laundry room, please.' Her voice, while outwardly pleasant, had a deeply unpleasant undertone, one brooking no refusal. Karen gently removed the two little ones from her lap, and stood up carrying Hijacker with her. 'Yes, Ma'am!' she couldn't resist snapping and Greta turned from where she was sorting sheet music.

'We've had him for quite a while now, and none of us have got sick from his germs,' she protested. 'If you don't want him by the little kids, let him come over here with me. I hate to think of him being locked up!' Her brow was creased as she pleaded for the seal.

'Greta, dear, I don't want him in here! Now please allow me to decide what's safest for you all. Anyone who wishes to visit him there, may do so at any time. Karen . . . please!'

Karen, wondering how long it would take Greta, who was not stupid, to think to ask why the seal's alleged germs would be safer in the laundry room than in the living room, made angrily for the door.

'Oh, Karen,' called Melissa, 'There're some bags of potato chips in the kitchen. Will you bring them here please? The children can have a little snack while I read them their story.'

Karen slammed the door. She couldn't help herself! But for all that, was not spared the tinkling laugh and Melissa saying, 'There goes mean old Karen, getting mad again! Never mind . . .'

Never mind what, Karen did not stick around to hear; she was on her way to her room to start packing!

The fact that her suitcases were on her bed, that her clothes were neatly folded in them and that she had already called the water-taxi company on the radio phone and ordered transportation for the next day, did nothing to ease the ache in her heart when she went to kiss the children goodnight as was her custom after they were in bed. She discovered that it was perfectly all right for her to have done all the work of unhooking, untying, unbuckling and unzipping, all the lifting in and out of tubs, the drying and powdering and dressing in pyjamas and lifting into beds, of bent bodies, but when it came to the actual 'goodnight' ritual which she, herself, had initiated, she was shoved right out!

In came Melissa, pockets bulging interestingly. 'Who do you want to tuck you in, my darlings?' she crooned to the youngest girls. 'Karen . . .' and although she had not said 'mean old' in front of it, it was tacitly there . . . 'or Auntie Melissa?'

'Auntie Melissa! Auntie Melissa!' the chorus went up, and was repeated in every other room she went to, and every room she left, she left cheeks full of candy sucked tightly against freshly brushed teeth. Karen ground her own teeth together, hating Melissa more with each breath she drew, each step she took and as each moment passed.

'I can't stand it!' she yelled at Hijacker, banging a pot-lid hard on the counter top. 'I just can't!' She slammed the lid down again and again, it felt so good! 'I'm getting out of here while I still can! I'd love to take you with me or at least turn you loose, but it'd break the kids' hearts to lose you!'

'Break them to lose you, too,' said an amused voice behind her. Don reached out, turned on the gas under the kettle and shoved Karen into a chair. 'Not thinking of leaving, are you?'

'I'm not just "thinking" of it. I'm doing it!' she snapped. 'I've packed and called for the water-taxi to pick me up tomorrow. And don't kid yourself, Don; the kids couldn't care less if I lived or died! They didn't even want me to k-kiss them g-goodnight!' Karen buried her face in her arms and bawled with as much lusty fury as one of the three year olds might have mustered.

'Kids get sick of a steady diet of candy,' he said comfortingly a few moments later having picked out some of the words she was saying in her rage.

'But do they get sick of hearing that Haida chiefs and sons of chiefs are too good to do dishes? Do they get sick of being taught to use make-up so they can make themselves "sexy" at thirteen and fourteen years of age to attract those same sons of chiefs? Do they get sick of having a pretty tinkling laugh floating around them all the time from a pleasant, good-natured woman who's never tired or grouchy or asking them to do chores? And just a few days ago Julie said I was s-sort of their m-mother!'

'So you're going to let her drive you away so Brent will never know you had guts enough to come here?'

'What choice do I have? I haven't got guts enough to go on staying! Anyway, he only asked me to come as a stop-gap until she would be free to come! It's not his fault I read more into his asking me to come than he meant me to!'

'Did you do that, Karen?'

'Yes! Yes, I was stupid enough to do that!'

'Oh . . . poor, poor, Karen. And she told you that you were to be a stop-gap, did she? That sounds like our baracuda.'

His sympathy when she was already feeling far too sorry for herself was too much for Karen and she got to her feet, tears running down her face. Don reached for her, drew her down onto his lap and pulled her face down onto his shoulder. 'Here,' he said, 'this is what shoulders were made for,' and when the door opened and Melissa's voice called out sharply, 'What is the meaning of your bags being packed?' Don kept Karen's face pinned down.

'Don't sweat it, Melissa,' he said inelegantly. 'She's going to unpack in a few minutes. We all have these little misunderstandings now and then and threaten to run home to Mama.'

'But . . . but. . . .' blubbered Karen a few minutes later, 'you made her think . . .'

'I did, didn't I?' he agreed complacently with a puckish grin. 'Won't hurt her a bit to think you have a champion, which indeed you do. I can't let you run away . . .' that phrase again! Karen thought . . . 'because if you do, she will no longer be the sweet, nice tempered "auntie" who hands out candies and kisses, but she'll become a tired, overworked drudge like someone else I could mention. I'm scared stiff that a tired, cranky Melissa would be a whole lot different from a tired, cranky Karen. And,' he added thoughtfully, 'if she weren't to be overworked and overtired, the only way she could avoid it would be to shove all the work off onto my Lou. If that happened, I'm afraid I'd have to get very, very obnoxious!'

Karen's eyes opened wide, a happy grin glowed across her face. 'Your . . . Lou?'

195

'In time,' he said heavily. 'I have to give her time, but I've given her an entire summer and it seems the idea still scares her. She won't talk to me, won't let me talk to her! She refuses to believe that I'm not just sorry for her. How could any man love her? She's ugly, didn't you know?'

'She is not!' Karen bristled quickly.

'Oh, come on, Karen! I know that! She's the one who doesn't!'

'Then you think if she weren't "ugly" you'd have a chance?' asked Karen eagerly, her mind working in full gear.

'I'd like to think so. You know her. What do you think?'

'I think I can talk her into some very necessary surgery. She asked me about it just tonight! And I think the girl's nuts about one school teacher who looks like he belongs in his own class-room!'

'But . . .' Don's face fell, making him look even younger. 'But you said you couldn't stay on here, that you'd had enough, and honestly, Karen, I can't blame you. If I were you, as soon as Brent's here to keep the baracuda in line, I'd be on the first boat out.'

'I'll stay until Lou goes for surgery. That much I promise you. And I'll try hard to make it soon.'

'Yes, Karen, try . . . try hard. I'm awfully partial to Christmas weddings and honeymoons.'

'A Christmas wedding and honeymoon? Yes, sir! I am yours to command!'

NINE

The banishment of the seal from all but the laundry room and kitchen may have been the reason, but Karen preferred to believe Don's theory that the return of the children to her 'sphere of influence' was caused by their suddenly becoming sickened by too much sweetness . . . both candy and the other kind. Greta was the first. She came the very next morning to see Hijacker and stayed to talk to Karen. She hesitated for a few minutes and then sheepishly asked if she could set the table, even though she had been one of the first to take advantage of Melissa's dictum that the children would do only what they pleased.

'I . . . I've been getting kinda bored,' she said, not meeting Karen's eyes. 'There's not too much to do around here.'

Margo, who had never totally abandoned Karen, was next. She flung herself through the door in the afternoon, skidded to a stop with squealing wheels and blew out a gusty sigh. 'I'm so sick,' she complained bitterly, 'of listening to dumb old Haida legends!'

Frankie was close enough behind her to hear and cut in on the conversation. 'Not as sick as I am! That Freddy's a pain! He's no fun anymore! You know, Karen, I timed Melissa and she said "really!" every fifteen seconds from the time Freddy started his last story until I walked out just now! We haven't worked on the model of the "Cuttysark" since she came!'

The next recidivists, which is what Karen felt sure Melissa would call them, were Julie, Mary and Lily, who, as a group, searched Karen out. 'Will you come and sing tonight, Karen? Greta said she won't play if you don't. She's tired of "Old Macdonald" and "There's a Hole in the Bottom of the Sea". We don't want to sing them anymore, either, or, "Row, Row, Row Your Boat".'

Karen realized later that it had not been such a good idea to listen to the kids' pleas, for Melissa had pouted prettily and sighed loudly and often enough to make some of the children, Francie and Flo, among the younger set, and Freddy, Big Peter and June in the older group, feel guilty. They started a counter-move in the form of a loud guitar accompanying 'Old

Macdonald', a song which, for some reason, Melissa liked and considered suitable for her 'darlings'. She did not like 'Yellow Submarine', 'Feelin' Groovy', or the one which Greta loved to belt out, 'Song of Joy', from Beethoven's Ninth.

When the counter-move began Karen quietly folded her tent and told her group that she had work to do. 'Why don't you join the others?' she suggested; she did not want any enemy camps forming, or dissent among the children.

Over the next couple of days, in twos and fours and singly, they returned, some seeking apples or other snacks, some seeking the seal, and all, whether they admitted it or not, seeking a return to the rapport they had shared with Karen before the advent of Melissa.

Although human nature made it hard for Karen not to listen to each and every new gripe against Melissa, in the interests of correct child-rearing practices, she determinedly choked them off while listening sneakily to childish chatter from which she learned a great deal when the kids didn't know she was hearing them. 'Unjustifiable eavesdropping!' Don called it with a grin when he caught her smirking outside a bedroom, but he stayed with her and listened, too! until they moved off to the kitchen to do a lot of laughing together.

Melissa, of course, did not give up without a struggle, and the more desperate she became, the more ridiculous she made herself appear to the very ones she was trying to impress, until even her most stalwart defenders were showing signs of disenchantment.

'There you are!' she cried gaily one evening as she found a large group in the kitchen with Karen. 'Oh, Frankie, darling! Your poor arms!' She wheeled to Karen, her eyes flashing angrily as she scolded her. 'How many times have I told you not to put these poor children to work? If it weren't for the fact that I need the small amount of help you provide me, or if I could hire someone to take your place, you'd be gone so fast your head would spin! Frankie, you are to stop that at once!'

Frankie kept doggedly turning the pestle in the ricer, watching the worms of crushed apple pulp squeeze out. 'I'm enjoying th ... .' he began but she cut him off, snatching his hand from the tool.

'Darling, you told me when I first arrived how you hated doing things like housework . . . I remember your saying it!

Now I don't know what kind of a hold Karen thinks she has over you, but believe me when I tell you you do not have to do this. She can't force you. I won't permit it! And Frankie, you promised you'd show me how your crystal-set works. You said it would be best on a clear night and there are a million stars out there!'

Pedantically, Big Peter said, 'You can only see a few thousand stars at one time. I read it in a book.' He reached for the ricer and took up where Frankie had left off.

'Please come, Frankie?' asked Melissa with a little pout. He sighed heavily and wheeled out in her wake, a dark frown on his face when he turned to say, 'Save some for me!' Whether it was a turn on the ricer to 'watch the squishy worms come out' or some of the apple butter they were making, Karen wasn't sure, but she sent him on his way with a warm smile.

Both Harry and George were still somewhat Melissa fans in their quiet, unassuming manner, and Karen hadn't really missed their presence; neither of them had been staunch Karen fans at any time, so she was quite surprised when they came to her one day and asked for the vacuum cleaner. 'Mr Edmund says he doesn't believe we can really use it together, like a team. C'n we show him?'

Don, straight-faced, refused to meet Karen's eye as the two, George holding the hose and pushing the nozzle, and Harry on his sticks shoving the machine along before him, cleaned the floor in the dining room immediately after lunch, much to Melissa's vociferous disgust.

'Karen you've been told! I will not have you demeaning these boys with girls' work!'

Don replied, cutting her off quite effectively with a jeering smile. 'Lady, if only girls are capable of housework, that makes them better men than boys are!' Frankie and Freddy, taking a dim view of Don's somewhat libelous statement, wrested the vacuum from the two younger ones and the 'sons of chiefs' ignored Melissa's glower until it changed to her tinkling laugh and she said lightly.

'Oh, I'm sure you're capable of it, boys, I didn't mean that! It's just that there are so many more manly things you could do!'

'Like what?' asked Freddy, rudely, bitterly. 'Hunt whales? Carve totems?' He gave a harsh laugh. 'Frank'd get the harpoon line stuck in his wheels and I'd chop up my sticks instead of the pole!'

Mike seemed vastly amused by this and roared, soon joined by his three room mates and the rest of the group. Don dragged his students off to class, two points having been made to everyones' satisfaction; crippled children can be useful around the house, and boys were just as capable as girls. The only loser seemed to be Melissa, and all she lost was her dignity as she swept from the room with gales of laughter chasing her angry figure. She would never believe that the kids had laughed, not at her, but at the picture conjured up by Freddy's words.

Matters were not improved, Don told Karen after dinner, when Mike, on three separate occasions during the meal had broken down into a heap of giggles, remembering, saying over and over, 'Watch that harpoon line! Freddy, don't chop your sticks!' until Melissa was frantic.

'I will not be made fun of!' she had snapped, according to Don. 'You are a very silly boy! Go to your room!'

Karen, who heard nothing of the story until quite late in the evening, had wondered at the loud titterings each time one of the children would scowl severely at another and say, 'You are a very silly boy!'

This soon became shortened to just plain, 'Silly boy!' in an affected manner and was equally as great a cause for mirth.

Each time Melissa heard the phrase she grew more and more tight-lipped, her tinkling laugh floated less freely and by the next day Karen was wondering if Melissa had ever had a sense of humour. If the older woman had showed no reaction, the boys would soon have forgotten the joke, but as it was they carried on until the shock and excitement of Louise's departure for an unheard of 'holiday' gave them a new point of interest and everyone, including Melissa and Mike, seemed to forget about the incident.

It had started, as far as Louise was concerned, the day a letter came for her with the week's supply of mail and groceries. 'But no one else has ever written to me!' she cried upon seeing that the handwriting was not Brent's. 'Who can it be from?'

She was with Karen and Don in the school-room. 'Open it and see, dummy,' said Don, shielding his laughing eyes from her view and exposing crossed fingers to Karen's sight. She grinned at him and whispered, 'Superstitions in teachers will not be tolerated!' He stuck out his tongue at her as Louise began reading:

' "Dear Louise,
You don't know us yet, but we feel we know you very well. We understand that you are thinking about having some plas . . ." '

She broke off, her face whitening, her eyes flying to the face of the teacher who was watching her intently. 'I'm not! I'm not! I don't know how these people got that idea! Karen . . .'

'Someone's calling me,' said Don and rushed out of the classroom to where the children were enjoying their morning recess outside.

'Lou . . . go on with your letter. You don't have to read it aloud.'

Louise shook her head, straightened out the crumpled page and took up where she had left off.

' ". . . plastic surgery done. We would be so pleased if you would consider staying with us while you visit the doctors and make arrangements, and then again, after your surgery, while you recuperate.

"Our children have all left home and we rattle around so, in this big house. You could have our youngest daughter's room for as long as you cared to stay.

"Talk this over with her again and let us know when to expect you." '

Her eyes widened with confusion. 'It's signed by "Frank and Diane Lytell" . . . who are they? Their youngest daughter? Talk it over with her again? The only person I ever talked to about it was . . .'

'Was Lytell's youngest daughter, Karen Jamison,' said Karen, as understanding dawned in Louise's face. 'When you told me you wanted to go, but didn't want to spend all that time in a hospital, that you'd miss the kids too much, I decided to make it easy for you. You do your recovering, not in a hospital, but in my home, and as for kids, I can supply them, too. My sister and her three live right next door, and my brother's a frequent visitor with his one. Now,' she challenged, 'what other objections can you think of?'

'I don't know them!'

'You know me. I know them. Would I send you to people who'd make you miserable?'

Louise shook her head. 'No . . . but do I have enough money?'

'What have you ever spent your wages on? The hospital won't cost you, room and board won't cost you. All you'll have to spend is what you want to, to fit yourself out with new clothes and a new hair style to go with your new face.'

Still Louise hesitated. 'I wish you could go with me!'

'Then who'd look after the kids? Lou, let me order a water-taxi for you, let me call my parents and ask them to meet you at Comox. You can take the bus up to Powell River and across from there to the island. Do it tomorrow, Lou!'

'Tomorrow? Oh, that's too soon! There's no time to think!'

'You've spent years thinking, love. You're going, Louise, and that's that!'

'But not tomorrow!'

'The day after, then!'

Louise wrapped her arms around herself, shivered and shook. 'Oh, Karen, I'm so *scared!*' she blurted. 'What if he won't . . .' She closed her eyes and shook her head rapidly back and forth, her jaws clenched.

'What if he won't still love you when you look the way you want to for him? What if all he really feels is pity and when you're no longer pitiable he finds someone else to pity?' Karen pushed the girl's arm. 'Lou, don't be an ass!'

Her beautiful eyes opened wide. 'Oh, gosh! You know everything! You're some kind of a witch! A mind-reader!'

'No,' chuckled Karen, knowing the battle was won, 'just another woman. You go, Lou-lou and let things like that take care of themselves one day at a time.'

Louise nodded, a new maturity on her face. 'The day after tomorrow.' It sounded like a solemn oath.

The only hitch they ran into was Melissa's stubborn refusal to allow Karen to use the radio phone in 'her' office, to make arrangements for Louise's departure.

'There is simply no need for that girl to have a vacation just now! She can wait until Brent comes back and hires more staff! The only reason you're sending her away is to give you more to do so the kids will have to help you! You'd do anything to lure them away from me!'

Karen was hardpressed not to shriek at her, to tell her that what Louise was having was not a vacation, but she had promised! No one, not Melissa, not the children, not a soul beyond Don and Karen were to know why Louise was going. She wanted to surprise Brent who had been after her for years to have the surgery. Louise wanted nothing more than to come home complete, or at least without an 'ugly' face and have him ask her who she was and Karen was determined to give the girl that opportunity, even though, as she laughingly told Louise, if she really expected to fool Brent, she had better wear a blindfold over her eyes.

So Karen refused to change her story that Lou needed a rest and would have a vacation no matter what Melissa thought. It was Don who had to storm the ramparts in the end, however, his physical superiority quickly overcoming Melissa's determination, and the calls were made amid the furious shrieks, heard even by the wondering children, that Brent would have Don fired the minute he returned and that as his return was a day overdue, Don had better start packing!

Young Mike capped it all as Don emerged from the office triumphantly rubbing his hands, by saying in a falsetto, 'Oh, Mr Edmund! You *are* a silly boy!' Don grabbed the boy, hustling him out and missed the malevolent glare which raked his back and was swung to Karen with the

hiss: 'You'll regret this!' Karen was to remember those words later.

The water-taxi came at first-light on the
great day. The children were all asleep as
Louise, Karen and the teacher crept out of
the house and down the walk to the float.
Louise clung to Karen for a long moment
before she turned to Don, hand extended,
trembling, and said, 'Good-bye, Mr
Edmund,' in a tiny, polite voice.

He took her hand, drew her close until
their bodies almost touched. 'Try again,
Lou.'

She swallowed hard, lowered her lashes
over luminous eyes full of unshed tears and
said, barely over a whisper, 'See you . . .
later . . . Don.' He turned and walked
swiftly away.

Karen watched while the boat gurgled
out; she waved once and then ran for the
house. The chilly air with a hint of frost
and the scent of smoke ruffled the golden
maple leaves and fluttered through the
scarlet of the dogwoods. She slipped grate-
fully back into her bed while the sound of
the departing boat faded and grew again,
making her wonder how the vagaries of the
echo-chamber of the inlet could make a
distant boat sound so near, but it wasn't

worth wondering about and she slid down the slope into sleep only to be jerked out of it, and her bed, seemingly an instant later by a terrible cry close at hand!

It came once more as she tugged her robe on and went to the hall, following the cries to Mike's bedside, where she found him sitting bolt upright trapped in the horrors of a nightmare.

'No, no, no! Don't tell him! Don't tell him to send me away! I'm sorry I was bad . . . no, no, no, no!'

'Mike, Mike! Hey! it's all right!' Karen sat on the side of his bed and pulled him against her as her voice woke him and he began to sob. 'What is it? Tell me, Mike.'

'The fire, the fire,' he howled. 'Don't tell on me! He'll send me away if you do, just like you sent Lou away! Oh, please! Don't tell! Don't tell!'

'Mike! For heaven's sake what are you talking about?'

'Yes,' rasped a harsh, weary voice in the doorway, 'What *is* he talking about?'

TEN

'Brent . . .' Karen's whisper was lost in the shouts of the boys.

'Quiet!' he hissed, 'It's not time to wake the household. Go back to sleep. I'll see you later.' To Karen he said harshly, 'I'll wait . . .'

She went to him, found him leaning tiredly against the wall across the hallway, his face a mask, his arms folded against his chest, his leg in a walking-cast jutting out, resting on its rubber heel. He was staring bleakly at her.

'What's going on here? When did you come? What's this fire, sending him away, sending Lou?' He steadied his voice with effort and said, 'God! I don't understand a thing!'

'Oh, Brent!' was all Karen could say as she moved to stand directly in front of him, unable to say anything else. Her mind, her heart, her entire being were so filled with love of him that all she felt could only be expressed in that one word, 'Brent!'

The look in his eyes was unreadable but his arms were no longer folded, they were reaching now, reaching for her and she was leaning toward him, her face lifted to his and he said, 'You . . . here! Are you real?' And a low laugh tinkled as light footsteps tripped down the hall and Melissa floated up to Brent, her scarlet caftan swishing. Karen stood back.

'Darling!' She squeezed his arm. 'I heard the boat and my heart leapt, thinking it was you, but then I remembered this was the day poor Lou was to leave so it wasn't until I heard your steps that I knew you were home! Oh, it's so good to see you . . . but you look so tired, Brent, and so bewildered! Darling, I couldn't tell you all the news over the radio so I had to keep it to myself . . .' She waved a hand in Karen's direction. 'Including this. She decided she couldn't stand being called a coward by even a casual acquaintance, and just plunked herself down to wait for you to come back!'

Brent seemed to sway and Melissa said, 'Oh, I'm so stupid, keeping you standing here like this. Come with me, darling, I have your apartment all ready and I'm going to cook breakfast for you before we say one single word more.'

With a look over his shoulder at Karen's set face Brent followed Melissa, leaving the other girl to wonder if, when he reached for her, he had been going to embrace her, or strangle her! The look on his face when he turned said it had been the latter and when Karen saw him next, her suspicions were confirmed.

'So,' he said quietly but with a note of bitter fury as he stared down at her like the eagle he was, 'So you called my bluff? Couldn't stand being called a coward and had to come to prove me wrong! It must have been a shock to find I wasn't here, and that if you wanted to prove anything, you'd have to wait! But that you could use innocent children as tools to get back at me is what I'll never forgive!

'It must have been hard on you to have to go to work and do the little you do. If I remember, hard work isn't your forte. Too bad you tried to throw your weight around and found yourself with the housekeeper's job. Well, it's your own fault, but it's the others it's hurting that makes me so sick! If it weren't for you Melissa wouldn't be exhausted trying to do the job of one nurse and three aides! I'm told you only intended to stay long enough to prove your point, but that's where you made your mistake! You called my bluff and now I'm calling yours! You'll stay until a full staff has come to replace the ones you drove out!'

'You're out of your mind!' Karen's head was reeling from the list of her 'sins'! 'You can't believe all that! If you do, you can't want me to stay! You can't force me, anyway!'

'Can't I? I won't take you and I'll keep you from calling in a water-taxi! You'll see how easily I can force you to stay!'

She flung back her head and faced him squarely. 'You believe that? You believe I only came to call your bluff? That I drove the housekeeper and aides away! What evidence do you have that any of that's true? Do you believe I haven't been pulling my own weight around here? Well, is that what you believe?'

'Yes! I have the evidence of my own eyes and ears! I saw the kids setting the table for breakfast! I heard Mike begging you not to send him away like you'd sent Louise! I asked Melissa about it and finally had to force the truth out of her! You sent her away for two reasons; one, so her influence over the kids would be gone and you could pass your chores off onto them and two, so you'd have a clear field with Don Edmund!'

'What?' Karen literally screamed the word at him and his fingers bit into her shoulder, crushing the bone to prevent the escape she was trying to make.

'And,' he went on relentlessly, 'I heard all about the fire you blame Mike for after it was you who gave him a candle in the first place!'

'That's not true! Brent! None of this is true! Oh, please, please listen to me!'

But, as once before when she had begged him to listen, he was striding off to fling open the door and almost bowl over the teacher who was entering, including Don in his look of utter contempt. Don, however, had no idea what had caused the look and was not to be put down. 'Hi, Boss, heard you were back! How's the leg?'

'Great,' snarled Brent. 'It'll be good enough by Christmas if you want me to be best man!'

'Karen,' said Don, greatly surprised. 'You told him?' and he totally missed the sardonic glance which lashed Karen as Brent said, 'Not true? None of it?' before he stumped off, in danger of breaking his cast.

'Hey, hey, hey,' said Don, touching Karen's cheek. 'What gives? I said the wrong thing at the wrong time or something?'

'Or something,' she agreed weakly. 'Oh, Don!' she groaned, 'Melissa must have overheard us talking about a Christmas wedding and honeymoon and she's told him it's you and I and you just came in and virtually confirmed it!' She sobbed once. 'He thinks I sent Lou away to give me a clear field with you!'

'He does, does he? Well I can bloody well tell him the truth, right now!'

Karen caught his arm. 'No, you can't! Don't you see? You'd have to tell him where Lou is and why and it'd spoil it all for her! Oh, Don, you know how much it means to her! Oh . . . who cares, anyway? Who's it going to hurt?' She slumped to a chair.

'You,' he said succinctly.

'So what? I told you I'd been stupid enough to think he wanted me here because he loved me, but he was only offering me a job. He loves Melissa.'

'So she says. Did he?'

'Just as good as. He believes everything she told him about me . . .'

When Don had heard the whole story he blew out a gusty breath. 'Well, looks like my favourite nightmare's coming true. I'm going to find out how a tired, cranky Melissa differs from a tired, cranky Karen. In a way, though, I'm glad. You'll be able to be with Lou. You will, or course, be leaving?'

'I will, of course, be staying! He won't let me go.'

'He must be nuts! He can't force you to stay!'

'That's what I told him. It seems he can and will, until he gets some staff here to replace the ones I "drove" away. Besides, I have to stay. I promised Lou.'

'She wouldn't hold you to that under the circumstances!'

'Maybe not, but like you say, if Melissa finds herself having to get her hands dirty, she'll make life pretty rough for the kids. No, I have to see this through.'

In a few days the wild excitement of Brent's return had died down and the children got back to normal. Normal being spending as much time with Karen as possible, but she was a different Karen, a warmly loving one, still, but quieter, more apt to want to be alone amid their chatter, needing their presence, but not wanting to be a part of the group.

The two tinies were with her nearly all day; they missed Louise terribly and turned to Karen. 'Karen love Jill?' asked one of the urchins who was squatting on the floor Karen was trying to scrub. 'Karen wuvs Tommy!' cried her counterpart, shoving her aside.

Karen grinned into their little gargoyle faces. 'I love you both, but you're getting your clean clothes dirty.'

'Love Tommy, love Jill?' asked Jill and Karen agreed patiently that she truly did, sliding them both along in front of her while she scrubbed where they had been sitting. 'Love Freddy? Love Frankie? Love Junie? Love Margo? Love . . .'

'I love all the kids, Jill!' said Karen to put a stop to the roll call. She leaned forward and planted a kiss on each little face. 'But I'd love you two a whole lot better if you'd move your little bodies out of my way. When I'm finished I'll take you to the swings if it's not raining by then.'

'I'll take them,' said Brent, startling Karen. She had not known he was leaning in the doorway watching her. 'Come on, you two.'

'No,' said Tommy, holding fast to Karen's floor rag. 'Karen go too. Karen push me, you push Jill.'

'I can push you both. Two hands, see?' Brent waggled them.

The child shook his head stubbornly. He looked at Jill for support and she pushed out her square little chin. 'Karen too!'

'Seems unanimous,' said Brent, scooping the two urchins out of her way. 'We'll wait for her to finish.'

I'll never be finished; she felt like telling him. When this is done there is laundry waiting, some beds need changing, meaning more laundry. The dusting isn't done, nor is the vacuuming! The windows are filthy and there are still two meals to prepare as well as baking which has to get done! But she said none of this, only worked doggedly on and when she was ready, accompanied him outdoors with the kids.

As she pushed Tommy gently to and fro she could feel Brent's eyes on her. She slid a glance at him. He looked angry. 'You're looking tired,' he commented.

'Sorry,' was her reply. 'I'll try not to.'

'Oh, for God's sake, I wasn't complaining, just remarking!'

'Oh.'

'You're making it damned hard for me to talk to you!'

'Sorry,' again. 'I didn't know you wanted

to talk. I thought you had just made a re-mark.'

She could actually hear his teeth grinding. 'Look, what I'm trying to say is you do too much! You should take it a bit easier!'

'It has to be done. If I put it off one day it's still there the next.'

He made no further comment and in a few minutes she lifted Tommy from the cage-like swingseat. 'That's all . . . I have to go. You can stay out here.'

'Karen wuv Tommy?'

'Karen loves Tommy . . . and Jill,' she added hastily.

'And Brent?' asked Tommy, but Karen was rushing away, pretending not to have heard.

She was folding sheets when he came in and said, 'I'm ordering you to go and have a cup of coffee, sitting down, with your feet up. Now move!'

'I want to get finished in here, damnit! Unless you don't want any dinner tonight?'

He tugged at the sheet she had just picked up, and her only alternative to let-ting go was to be pulled close to him. She let it go. 'I'll finish this,' he said firmly. 'You do what you're told!'

Still, she hesitated, and when he said in a strained voice, 'Karen . . . I'm warning you!' she fled, and sat down with a cup of coffee, put her feet on another chair and laid her head back, closing her eyes against the stinging behind them. Why did he have to do that? Why didn't he just leave her to get on with her work? She didn't want him to help, didn't want him to care that she was tired, but oh! how good it felt to know that he did!

'Now it's almost cold,' he said gently and she opened her eyes to see him looking down at her. 'Drink it, Karen. Please!' And he sounded so fierce and tender that she nearly wept, and might have, might have thrown herself against him, clung as he looked like he wanted her to cling, and told him how tired she was, how Melissa had lied about her, was still lying, how she did not love Don, but loved him, Brent, and . . .

'There you are! I've been looking all over for you,' cried Melissa, coming through the door with a basket over her arm. 'Come here, please, darling, and let me measure this against you.' She drew out a nearly completed section of sweater and held it against Brent, her hands smoothing it over his shape. 'Hmm, another few inch . . .' She gasped as the knitting was almost torn out of her hands and the needles went

223

flying as a madcap seal rolled over and over, wrapping himself in yarn which was coming, not only from the ball which had fallen and attracted his attention, but from the knitting Melissa was trying desperately to retain.

'Stop him! Stop him!' she shrilled, stamping her foot as her work continued to unravel. 'Brent! Do something!'

But Brent was roaring with laughter, shouting 'Look at him go! Oh, just look at him go!' so it was Karen who grabbed the seal and quickly broke the yarn leading to the unravelling sweater. She began gently to untangle Hijacker from the wool he was wrapped in and, still laughing, Brent came to help her. Melissa kept up her running tirade against the seal and the stupidity of people who kept such animals in the house until Brent said, 'Oh, knock it off, 'Liss! If you'd broken the wool like Karen did instead of standing there screaming, your work wouldn't have been unwound. Anyway, you can do it again; what else do you have to do?'

'What else? Brent! A thousand things! The children to care for, to entertain, to put to bed, to get up in the mornings, the house to oversee!' With that she stalked out, leaving Karen to cope with the tangle of yarn.

Brent took Hijacker back to the laundry room. 'I'm sorry I forgot to shut the door.'

'It's all right. He's supposed to have the run of the kitchen. I'm sorry Melissa was upset. You'd better go and make your peace with her.'

'No . . . I'm going to help you with those beds.'

'There's only three left. I can manage, or if I don't get time, Don'll help me when school's out . . .'

'What'll I help you with? School is out.' said Don, entering and pushing Julie ahead of him.

'I made Karen take a break and spoiled her schedule. She has some beds to do.'

'Sure I'll help.' He chucked Karen under the chin. 'Don't I always?'

Brent left without a word, not even one for Julie who stared after him, hurt. 'That baracuda's making him mean, too,' she said, and Don and Karen exchanged a quick, guilty look. When had the kids heard that?

'That's not a nice thing to say,' Karen admonished severely as a group of other children crowded into the room, pushing and shoving to get near the table.

'What's not a nice thing?' asked Margo.

'Baracuda,' said Julie innocently. 'Is it worse than witch or dragon?'

Karen spluttered into her cold coffee, coughed and managed to bring herself under control enough to hear Don say, 'But you only called the other two names among yourselves, not in front of us. I don't recommend you get overheard using that term, any of you!'

'But we called them that to you!'

'Only after they were gone,' said Karen, 'and couldn't be hurt by it. Now let's drop the subject and have no more name-calling! You guys better report to the living room. I'm sure Brent and Melissa are waiting for you.'

'Aw, Karen . . .' and 'Do we hafta?' were heard over Joey's saying, 'Hey, Karen, that's a funny thing I was going to ask you about but I forgot until you said about the witch and the dragon being gone. When I said that you came before the b . . . before Auntie Melissa and after the witch left, Brent said little kids had no sense of time. But I do, don't I? I know when you came and the same day the dragon left and then a long time later she came. I know about time!'

'Sure, Joey, you have a remarkable sense

of time, and if I don't start dinner, you'll be telling me it's time long before it's ready. Why don't you help Mr Edmund with the beds and let me get on with it. Margo, Greta, take the others to the living room.'

'I was just coming for them,' said Brent, looking very hard at Karen. To the kids he said, 'Melissa has a bingo game all set up for you, so let's go.'

The next day Brent washed windows while Karen vacuumed and dusted. The day after, he peeled potatoes for her and scrubbed out all the tubs and shower stalls, and the day after that he took Tommy and Jill off her hands so she could have half an hour to herself.

'I wish they'd taken to Melissa better and would spend some time with her,' he complained.

'They might if they hadn't been firmly convinced I'm an ogre,' was the icy remark made as the woman under discussion entered the living room. For once Brent did not swing an accusatorial eye to Karen, but said quietly. 'I think you're making a mistake about that, 'Liss. I've heard both Don and Karen shut the kids up if they talk out of turn, so I can't believe they'd tell the babies you're an ogre.'

'Of course they shut the kids up when you're around. Neither of them is stupid.'

'Thanks for that,' Karen couldn't resist saying, even though she knew she could be earning disapproval from Brent by being sarcastic to Melissa. 'I hear the kids out for recess. I'll take my free half an hour with Don.' She stepped around Brent, leaving him to answer Melissa. His reply surprised her.

'They didn't even know I was around,' he said, and sounded just as disenchanted as Freddy sometimes had in the days when he was ceasing to be a Melissa fan.

Did that mean he had heard all that business about the baracuda . . . and all the rest of it? And did it mean he was beginning to wonder if maybe Melissa was not always quite truthful?

It seemed not, she reflected a day or two later when, dusting the floor outside the office, she heard him on the radio phone talking to Mr Hobbs.

'. . . don't want anyone young,' he was saying. 'No, Mr Hobbs, if she's not a middle aged, motherly type, she's not the housekeeper I want. And while you're at it, how about advertising for three aides, also middle aged and motherly, or even L.P.N.s, if need be. I'm sure the foundation can afford them.'

'Licenced Practical Nurses run to quite a bit more than aides,' said the tinny voice over the loud speaker. 'Why not one L.P.N. and another R.N. if you don't think aides can do the job?'

'I have one perfectly wonderful R.N.,' said Brent, 'but she needs help. However, I want that housekeeper sooner than yesterday!'

At that point Karen took off, thinking about the old adage regarding eavesdroppers.

It was a Saturday morning and Karen was in the kitchen baking apple pies with a large audience and a few helpers. Brent came in.

'What's the attraction in here?' he asked somewhat testily.

'Makin' pies,' someone answered.

'There's a movie set up. It came yesterday with the mail, so if you want to see it, hurry up!'

There was utterly no sign of hurry among the children. 'What is it, "Snow White" or "Cinderella"?' asked Big Peter. Then, without waiting for a reply, he said,

'Toss me one of those, Frankie, and I'll peel it.'

Frankie tossed him an apple which he missed and it bounced to the floor in front of Hijacker who thought a game had started. He chased the apple, caught it and threw it. It landed on the table and in a flash he was up and over the wheel of George's chair, onto the table, knocking over a bowl of peeled fruit, rolling through Karen's pie dough and flipping the flour canister to the floor in a puffing white cloud which made the children cough and beat at their clothes.

With a whoop, Brent was after him, catching Hijacker in a flying tackle and rolling across the floor with him, cast bumping along as he hooted in triumph, short lived triumph, for the seal was as crafty as he was slippery and in an instant had shot free to leap from Brent's chest to a chair and to the top of the counter where he met up with the spice cans once more and sent them flying, one catching Melissa smack in the mouth as she saw Brent on the floor and screamed.

The seal, startled, flopped off the counter and landed on Brent, who was laughing too hard to take evasive action. Melissa tore through the crowd of semihysterical children, still screaming, and struck out at Hijacker with both hands, crying out, 'Get off! Get off, you horrible little brute!' She tried to grab him by his really nonexistent neck and when that failed, tugged viciously at one of his flippers as Brent rolled over in an attempt to to protect the seal. Hijacker objected to having his flipper pulled and his sharp white teeth snapped at air a fraction of an inch from Melissa's hand. With a scream of rage she snatched up a long, sharp knife from the table and plunged it toward him.

The seal swerved sinuously and the knife gleamed wickedly as it sliced into Brent's shoulder.

Melissa screamed once more and fainted.

Karen tore the shirt away and looked, saying soothingly, 'It's not too bad. Just a nick,' as much for the childrens' sake as for his, although he was white and shocked. 'Come on and I'll clean it up for you.' She snatched a clean tea towel which had just been ironed and covered his bloody shoulder, keeping pressure on it as she walked him out of the room, saying to Don, who had just entered, 'Take over in here.'

'There's a very complete medicine kit in my apartment. That thing needs stitches, doesn't it?'

Karen swallowed hard. 'Yes. We could call for a doctor to fly in . . .'

'No. You can do it.'

He sat on the edge of the tub and watched her as she cleaned his wound, saw her face grow paler and paler each time she had to push the needle in and out of his skin; there had been no anaesthetic in the 'complete' medical kit, and when she had tied the last knot in the last of the eight sutures she was limp, exhausted, her face streamed sweat and there was blood on her lip where she had bitten it. She made no protest when he pulled her down onto his knees and pushed her face against his good shoulder, stroking her hair and murmuring, 'No . . . Ah, Karen, don't . . . It's all right . . . you didn't hurt me.'

She shuddered and shuddered and shuddered and when he lifted her face to wipe it with a towel, to look into her eyes and say, 'Oh, God, how I love you!' and cover her trembling mouth with his own, she could only press closer and closer, clinging, moaning, her fingers tangling in his hair.

When at last he lifted her away from him and took her into his living room to sit on the sofa, a much better place for making love than the edge of a tub, she did not want to meet his eyes. He forced her to. 'Casual acquaintance? God! How that hurt! Why, Karen-mine? Why?'

'She said it first. She said when she came that you had told her about me, a "little widow" you'd met casually on vacation and felt sorry for and offered a job. You told her all about me. You laughed with her about me! About how women you try to treat fall in love with you. You think that didn't hurt?'

'An unnecessary hurt, sweetheart. I didn't laugh about you!'

'But you told her!'

'I told her . . . asked her to find you! I thought a nurse would know how to go about finding another nurse and when she called me with your address I left here and went for you. I was going to bring you here by force if necessary and I was driving too fast and had the accident. She said she'd come here to take over until I got back and then I was late coming back because I was looking for you. No one knew where you were! Except her, Karen-mine, and she didn't tell me! She says she didn't because you had made it clear you only came in answer to a challenge. To prove a point!'

'I came because I love you and where you are is where I have to be.'

A long time later he said, 'Get off my shoulder, woman. Those sutures weren't put in by an expert and if you pop 'em, I'll do without. I'll never put you through such hell again, even though that's what told me you love me.'

A sunbeam came through the curtains, struck Karen's hair and he lifted a strand, letting it trickle down. 'Wet cobwebs,' he reminded her.

At that moment a cry went up outside, was picked up and repeated until from the babble of voices Karen made out the words, 'Jewel Tree! Jewel Tree!' She looked her question at Brent.

'Come on!' He towed her out quickly, explaining as they rushed, 'It's something very special. We have our own little ceremony for it.'

The children, large, medium, small and tiny were standing there, their faces aglow with a kind of awed wonder blended with pleasure and belief in miracles. 'Look,' whispered Brent, but there was no need, for Karen was staring just as awed as any of the children at the small, leafless tree spangled and be-decked with beads of water, the sun slanting down through a break in the clouds to capture each droplet and turn it into an irridescent jewel until the entire tree glistened and sparkled with rubies and diamonds, sapphires, emeralds and aquamarines, decking it out with jewels from the gods.

Brent clasped the hand of the child nearest him as solemnly all hands were joined and faces were lifted. 'Greta . . . start us, please,' he said quietly. 'Sing to the tree.'

There was dead silence as all eyes were wrenched from the glory before them to rest on Karen's face. Julie said, 'Brent, we can't! The jewel song was sung at the funeral of our baby sister and it makes us sad.'

'Your . . . what?' he asked, mystified.

'Greta,' said Karen urgently, 'help me! I can't do it alone . . .' and the two clear voices rang out:

'When He cometh, when He cometh,
To make up His jewels,
All His jewels, precious jewels,
His loved and His own . . .'

They were joined by the others with,

'Like the stars of the morning,
His bright crown adorning,
They will shine in their beauty
Bright gems for His crown . . .'

As the voices faded out so did the sunbeam and a gentle puff of wind came to harvest the jewels but there was no grief for all the children knew there would be other days and other jewels . . .

Brent drew Karen aside, tilted her face up to his and said, 'Karen . . . ?'

'Yes,' she whispered. 'I was going to tell you about her, but . . .'

'But I made it impossible. And I call myself a psychologist! Sweetheart . . .' He swallowed hard and shook his head, straining her close to him.

'You were enough of a psychologist to make sure I knew the name of the place I was "supposed" to stay away from.'

'I was?'

'In your horrible little note!'

'Did I? I thought Melissa had told you!'

'Brent, I never laid eyes on Melissa until she arrived . . . a week before you were due. When I finally found the place there was no one here but Mrs Muffin and she only stayed a few hours.'

'I heard . . . but I thought the little kids had their times mixed up. Because they love you best, you must have been here longer . . . And you had this place all on your own! You walked in here cold and took over everything and I let her call you lazy! Oh, Karen-mine I have such a lot to make up to you!'

He was gazing enraptured into her face when Freddy called out plaintively, 'Will you hurry up and kiss her before this dumb Margo breaks all my fingers off?'

EPILOGUE

It was a cold, frosty morning in late November. The fog had just begun to lift from the still, black waters of the inlet when a boat nosed tentatively into the bay, sidled up to the float and three figures stepped off.

'It's a man and two ladies,' reported a watcher at a window. 'Hey, there goes Mr Edmund. He's running! Hey, you guys, he's . . . my gosh! He's kissin' one of the ladies!'

Karen, rapidly followed by Brent, flew from the house to meet her parents on the ramp. 'It's unbelievable! I never dreamed you'd bring her home! Oh, it's so good to see you!' she cried, hugging them both before introducing Brent.

'We had to come,' smiled Diane, 'and meet our new son-in-law.' She looked in amazement at the crowd of children staring down from the porch above. 'I can see now why you couldn't come home to get married. Baby sitters *must* be a problem!'

Over the ensuing laughter Karen heard a

soft cough behind her and turned to gaze at the young woman who stood with Don. Her hair, in a soft, shoulder-length pageboy, shone with good health. Her luminous eyes glowed with an etherial beauty and a tremulous smile quivered on her red mouth.

'Hi,' she said shyly, clinging to Don's hand as if she'd never let it go.

She released him, however, when Karen reached for her and hugged her tightly, fighting back tears of joy. Karen realized she was fighting a losing battle when Brent said, with a quizzical smile, 'Who's the girl, Don? Someone you met last summer?'